For more than forty years,
Yearling has been the leading name
in classic and award-winning literature
for young readers.

Yearling books feature children's
favorite authors and characters,
providing dynamic stories of adventure,
humor, history, mystery, and fantasy.

Trust Yearling paperbacks to entertain,
inspire, and promote the love of reading
in all children.

The Five Ancestors

THE fiVE ANCEStORS

猴 # Monkey

Jeff Stone

A YEARLING BOOK

for Tristen and Owen,
my little monkeys.

Published by Yearling, an imprint of Random House Children's Books
a division of Random House, Inc., New York

Visit us on the Web! www.randomhouse.com/kids

www.fiveancestors.com

Educators and librarians, for a variety of teaching tools, visit us at
www.randomhouse.com/teachers

ISBN-13: 978-0-375-83074-7
ISBN-10: 0-375-83074-X

Reprinted by arrangement with Random House Books for Young Readers

Printed in the United States of America

September 2006

10

The Legend continues . . .

Five young warrior monks have survived the destruction of Cangzhen Temple. Each is a master of a different fighting style, and each is appropriately named. Disappearing into the forest, the five are determined to follow their Grandmaster's instructions to seek out the secrets of the past.

But one year before, an older boy was exiled from Cangzhen. Also a master, he swore he was *not* appropriately named. It is this boy who has led the massacre and vowed vengeance on his former temple brothers. He will not rest until he has killed those destined to be . . .
the Five Ancestors.

Henan Province, China
4348 – Year of the Tiger
(1650 AD)

PROLOGUE

For the first time in a thousand years, there was thun-der in the temple.

Hidden inside the heavy terra-cotta barrel at the back of the practice hall, eleven-year-old Malao flinched with every BOOM, every CRACK! Thunder inside their compound could only come from one source. A dragon. A very angry dragon.

Malao shivered. According to legend, dragons controlled the wind and the rain, the lightning and the thunder. Stay in a dragon's good graces, and your crops would receive enough rain for a bountiful harvest; anger a dragon, and your crops would be washed away—along with you, your house, and your entire family. Push a dragon too far, and it would deliver a special kind of storm, smashing everything it could with its powerful tail, igniting everything that remained with its fiery breath.

A dragon must be the reason Grandmaster had made Malao and his four "temple" brothers—Fu, Seh, Hok, and Long—squeeze into the barrel. Grandmaster had told them they were under attack by soldiers, but Malao knew men alone could never defeat the warrior monks of Cangzhen Temple. The attackers must have formed an alliance with a dragon. What could those thunderclaps be but the crack of a dragon snapping its enormous tail?

A dragon lashing its tail reminded Malao of his older brother Ying and his chain whip. Ying had left Cangzhen in a rage the year before, upset because he had been trained his entire life as an eagle but had always wanted to be an all-powerful dragon. Swinging his chain whip was the closest Ying had ever come to having a dragon tail of his own.

Malao shivered again. Ying had vowed to return to Cangzhen to punish Grandmaster for training him as an eagle, but Ying was no fool. He would never attack Cangzhen and its one hundred warrior monks unless he was guaranteed victory. And for that to happen, he would have to have acquired power beyond that of mortal men—

Oh, no! *Malao thought.* Maybe Ying has figured out a way to transform himself into a real dragon! Maybe he has grown scales and a tail and—

KA-BOOM!

CHAPTER

1

Malao raced through the moonlit treetops, nervous energy driving him deeper and deeper into the forest. He had to put as much distance between himself and Cangzhen Temple as possible. Ying *had* returned— and was more dangerous than ever.

Malao leaped off the gnarled arm of an ancient oak and soared through the night sky.

He landed on the limb of a young maple and paused. He was lucky to be alive, let alone to have escaped uninjured. The same was true for his brothers Fu, Seh, Hok, and Long. Cangzhen Temple was in ruins, and its warrior monks—Malao's older brothers and teachers—were all dead.

Malao began to tremble. The thunder he had

heard was a devastating new weapon called a *qiang*. With the twitch of a single finger, a soldier with no training at all could now kill a kung fu master. Ying carried a *qiang,* and with it the power of a dragon. Still, that hadn't been enough for Ying. He had carved his face and filled the grooves with green pigment. He had forked his tongue and ground his teeth and nails into sharp points. Ying now looked like a dragon. A crazy, vengeful sixteen-year-old dragon.

Malao shuddered and grabbed hold of a thick vine. He pushed off the slender maple and swung feetfirst toward a large elm.

"Scatter into the four winds and uncover Ying's secrets, as well as your own," Grandmaster had told them. *"Uncover the past, for it is your future."*

Malao released the vine and somersaulted onto one of the elm's upper limbs. *Why did Grandmaster hide only us five?* he wondered. *What makes us so special?*

Grandmaster had provided only one clue. He'd said that Malao and his four brothers were linked to each other, and to Ying. Malao guessed it had something to do with the fact that all of them, including Ying, were orphans. Still, that didn't explain much. It wasn't like any of them could have had the same parents. They were all too different.

Malao glanced down at his small, dark hands. He was a monkey-style kung fu master, nothing at all like Fu, the oversized, over-aggressive twelve-year-old "tiger," or Seh, the tall, secretive twelve-year-old "snake."

He differed even more from Hok, the pale-skinned, logical twelve-year-old "crane," and Long, the wise, muscular thirteen-year-old "dragon."

Malao sighed. He missed them already.

A twig snapped and Malao froze. He glanced around but couldn't see anything from high in the tree. Cautiously, he swung down to the elm's lowest limb for a closer look. He peeked through a clump of new foliage and his heart skipped a beat. This part of the forest looked awfully familiar. His plan had been to travel in a straight line away from the temple, but he'd always been really bad with directions—

Another twig snapped.

Malao crouched low on the large limb and held his breath. A moment later, he saw a soldier on patrol. One of Ying's soldiers.

Malao shivered. He'd run in a big circle, and now he was right back where he'd started, near Cangzhen!

The soldier was headed in Malao's direction. Malao watched him closely. Heavy armor covered the man's body, and he carried a short wooden stick about as long as Malao's arm. Malao got a good look at the stick as the soldier passed through a pool of moonlight. The stick was nearly as big around as a monk's staff and was made from a very light-colored wood, white waxwood. The entire surface was decorated with intricate carvings that had been colored brown with a hot piece of metal. The soldier was still some distance away, but Malao knew exactly what those carvings were.

Monkeys.

Malao's upper lip curled back.

The warrior monks of Cangzhen Temple—or any temple, for that matter—were not allowed to have personal possessions. Personal possessions meant a tie to the greedy world of men, so the monks owned nothing and shared everything. However, within Cangzhen, weapons were an exception. Though they weren't supposed to favor any one more than another, Cangzhen's warrior monks almost always did. Malao's favorite was called a short stick, and the specific stick he preferred was now in that soldier's right hand.

Malao hugged his knees tight and began to rock back and forth. That soldier had helped slaughter Malao's friends and family and burn down the only home Malao had ever known. And now the soldier planned to walk away with a souvenir. Malao wasn't about to let that happen.

As the soldier passed under his tree, Malao focused on the rhythm of the soldier's strides. When the soldier's right arm went backward and his weight shifted to his left leg, Malao dropped from the tree like an anvil.

THUD!

Malao's feet smashed into the back of the soldier's left knee and the knee buckled, slamming to the ground. Malao grabbed the stick and flipped forward, twisting it out of the soldier's hand and leaping onto a low-lying branch. He grinned at the soldier and waved the stick.

"Get down here, you little monkey!" the soldier said, staggering to his feet.

Malao shook his head and scurried to a higher branch.

"Don't play games with me, monk. I see your orange robe. You better not make me climb up there after you."

Malao turned to leap to another tree when the soldier raised his voice. *"I said get down here!"*

Malao stopped. If the soldier raised his voice any louder, reinforcements might come. Malao had no interest in fighting an entire garrison of soldiers. He needed to do something, fast. He zipped to the opposite side of the tree so that he was directly behind the soldier, facing the same direction as the man, and jumped straight down. He landed with one small foot on each of the soldier's shoulders.

The surprised soldier tilted his head up and grabbed on to Malao's robe. Malao slipped his stick under the soldier's chin, pressed his knee against the base of the soldier's head, and leaned back.

The soldier choked and teetered backward, letting go of Malao's robe. He swung his arms wildly, trying to knock Malao off his shoulders. Malao responded by shifting his weight forward.

The soldier toppled over, hitting the ground face-first. He struggled, but Malao held the stick firm until the man's body relaxed. Malao slid the stick out from under the soldier and rolled him over.

The soldier was breathing slow and steady. Cautiously, Malao rested one of his bare, dark-skinned feet on the man's nose and wiggled his toes. The man didn't flinch.

The soldier was definitely unconscious.

Malao giggled softly and slipped his stick into the folds of his robe. He paused and looked around. Cangzhen was close. He might as well check to see if any of his brothers had circled back. Perhaps he could even spy on Ying and "uncover some of his secrets," as Grandmaster had instructed.

Grandmaster!

The last time Malao had seen Grandmaster, he'd been alone with Ying inside the burning practice hall. Those two would probably fight until only one was left standing!

Malao darted forward, silently following the soldier's tracks back toward Cangzhen.

CHAPTER 2

Inside the smoke-filled practice hall, student and master stood toe to toe in a fight to the death. Flames rolled like waves over the rafters high above, casting shadows across Ying's carved face. His black eyes burned hotter than the fire overhead. He popped his knuckles one at a time.

Grandmaster stood solid as an eighty-year-old oak.

"You know the real reason I've returned, don't you, old man?" Ying spat.

"From the look in your eyes, I can tell," Grandmaster replied.

"I hate you!"

"I know."

Ying spread his arms wide like an eagle and began

to circle Grandmaster. "Why did you raise me to be something I'm not?" he said.

"I thought it was best," Grandmaster said in a calm tone. His head turned slowly, his eyes following Ying.

"Best for who?" Ying snapped.

"Best for me, I suppose," Grandmaster replied. "Cangzhen needed an eagle. Perhaps I should have chosen something else. Something less . . . aggressive."

"Then what should you have raised me to be?" Ying asked sarcastically. "A dog to follow you around and jump at your every command? You should have raised me as I was meant to be raised!"

Grandmaster shook his head. "No, that would have been disastrous. Of that I am certain."

"You will pay for robbing me of my birthright!" Ying said. "And you will pay for changing my name. Others shall pay, too. My vengeance will fall on every person whose life you touched with warmth and compassion, for that is my destiny."

"That is indeed your destiny," Grandmaster said. "But you have the power to change it."

"Never!" Ying shouted. He stopped circling and stood behind Grandmaster. "After my man retrieves the dragon scrolls from your library, I will learn what I was born to learn. And when I close the final scroll, I will take with pride the name my father gave me. The name you tried to bury beneath the feathers of an eagle. Arrogant fool!"

"Do not follow in your father's footsteps," Grandmaster said. "I urge you to forge your own path. Your father was a sick man. Only a sick man would give his son the name—"

"ARRRGH!" Ying lunged straight at Grandmaster's back. His pointed teeth stopped a hair's breadth from Grandmaster's thin, wrinkled neck. "Don't you dare talk about my father that way!" Ying hissed. "He did nothing wrong, and you know it. It was all your doing. You set the events in motion, and you've been trying to reverse your wrongs ever since. That is why you took me away from the clan and raised me yourself, isn't it?"

"No," Grandmaster replied, turning to face Ying. "I took you in because I wanted to give you hope."

"You didn't take me in," Ying said. "You *took* me. You did it because you wanted to rewrite my future. Admit it!"

"I did it because I felt sorry for you," Grandmaster said, folding his bony hands. "And because I feared what you might become if you were exposed to the wrong people."

"*Exposed to the wrong people?*" Ying said. "You mean people with *passion*? People with *vision*? People like the Emperor?"

"Yes."

"Then you should never have taken me along to help him last year, you foolish—"

"I know," Grandmaster said, turning away. "I know. . . ." He lowered his head.

"Turn around and fight, old man!" Ying said.

Grandmaster shook his head.

Ying snarled and stepped around in front of Grandmaster. Grandmaster closed his eyes and turned away again.

"Face me!" Ying demanded.

Grandmaster raised his head high but said nothing.

Ying took a deep breath, rooting himself to the earth. "Then prepare to meet your ancestors. . . ."

Ying raised both hands ceremoniously and extended his fingers. Slowly he brought his fingers together and curled them down while stretching his thumbs down and curling them up. He snapped the perfectly formed eagle-claw fists back and drew a lifetime's worth of angry energy from every corner of his body, pushing it up through his shoulders, into his arms. Driven by hate, he slammed his clawlike fists into Grandmaster's back. There was a tremendous *CRUNCH,* and Grandmaster slumped to the floor.

Ying spat and walked out of the burning practice hall without bothering to give his father's killer a parting glance.

Malao slowed as he approached the tree line across from the Cangzhen compound. He picked a large maple and scurried up the trunk. Peeking through the new leaves at the end of a branch, he saw Ying standing in the smoky moonlight, just inside Cangzhen's main gate. A circle of soldiers surrounded Ying. Even from a distance, Malao could sense Ying's anger and hear bits and pieces of his ranting.

Ying seemed most upset with a man he called Tonglong, who looked to be about thirty years old and had an extraordinarily long, thick ponytail.

Nice haircut, Malao thought, and giggled to himself as he watched Tonglong formally present his straight sword to Ying. Ying unsheathed the sword and swung it dramatically over Tonglong's bowed head. Then he reached down, lifted a large, round object, and threw it at Tonglong.

Tonglong caught the spinning object and placed it on the ground, next to his feet. As Tonglong wiped his hands across his chest, Malao stared at the object. He couldn't figure out what it was. He thought there might be something else on the ground near Ying, but the soldiers were blocking his view. Malao scratched his head and looked back at Tonglong.

Malao knew *Tonglong* meant "praying mantis" in Cantonese Chinese. He also knew how rare it was for people in their region to have a Cantonese name. Most people spoke Mandarin Chinese.

Malao wondered how Tonglong got his name. Malao and his four brothers all happened to have Cantonese names—thanks to Grandmaster—and each was named after his spirit animal. The same was true for Ying. *Malao* meant "monkey" in Cantonese. *Ying* meant "eagle." A praying mantis seemed like an odd spirit animal to Malao, yet it suited Tonglong perfectly. He had a strange, insect-like quality.

For some reason, Malao couldn't take his eyes off Tonglong. It may have been the way the smoke mixed with the moonlight, but Tonglong reminded Malao of someone. . . .

Malao shook his head and tried to focus on something else. He stared at the object on the ground again. The smoke cleared for a moment, and Malao noticed that the large, round object was flesh-colored and streaked with red. It was someone's head! And it looked a lot like—

"*Grandmaster!*" Malao gasped.

"Hush," a voice whispered from behind Malao.

Malao jumped. He turned and saw his brother Hok on a limb behind him.

"Hok! Did you see—"

"Not here, Malao. Follow me."

Malao watched Hok drift silently through the trees, his robe fluttering against his slender frame like orange kite paper. Malao swallowed hard and followed.

Hok stopped in the forked limbs of an enormous, half-dead elm. The dead half had a large hollow in its massive trunk, high off the ground. Hok eased inside. Malao scurried in after him.

"Greetings, little brother," Hok whispered as he sat down. "I apologize for sneaking up on you like that. I hope I didn't scare you."

"D-don't worry about it," Malao stammered. "Did you see that? Grandmaster's head—"

"I know," Hok said. "It's over now. Sit."

"Over?" Malao said as he began to pace. "You call *that* over? We have to do something! We—"

Hok raised a pale hand. "Slow down, Malao. Please. We'll act when the time is right, but now is not the time. Why don't you take a deep breath and tell me what else you saw?"

Malao took a deep breath and exhaled slowly. He sat down across from Hok. "I didn't see anything else,"

Malao sighed. "I was only in the tree a moment before you came. How long have you been back?"

"Not long enough, unfortunately," Hok said. "I wish I had returned sooner. Perhaps I could have helped Grandmaster . . . or Fu."

Malao's eyes widened. "Fu?"

"Yes," Hok said. "After I circled back here, I saw Fu arguing with Ying at the main gate. Grandmaster was there, too. Ying sliced Fu's cheek pretty badly with his chain whip. Then he killed Grandmaster."

"*Ying* killed Grandmaster?" Malao asked.

"Yes," Hok said. "He sent a lead ball through Grandmaster's heart with a *qiang*."

Malao shivered and lowered his head. "P-please don't tell me any more."

"I'm sorry, little brother," Hok replied. He leaned toward Malao and his voice softened. "Let me tell you about Fu. He got away. I chased after him to see if I could help in some manner, but I never managed to catch up."

Malao sniffled and looked up. "Huh? You couldn't catch Fu?"

Hok shook his head and grinned. "No. I never imagined Fu could run so fast. I think he may have the dragon scrolls."

"That must be why Ying is so upset," Malao said.

Hok nodded slowly. "I think you're right."

"What happened to Fu?"

"I don't know. When it became clear that I could not catch him, I decided to head back here to learn more about what Ying was up to. That's when I saw you on the tree limb." Hok shook a finger playfully at Malao. "You really should have hidden yourself better, you know."

Malao rolled his eyes. "Give me a break. I'm wearing an orange robe and orange pants." He grinned.

Hok smiled back.

Malao looked at the moonlight reflecting off Hok's pale, bald head and said, "Do you know anything about that soldier Tonglong? The one with all the hair?"

"I think he may be Ying's number one soldier," Hok said. "And I have a feeling he made some kind of big mistake that allowed Fu to obtain the scrolls. Ying seemed to put most of the blame on him."

"Yeah, I heard Ying shouting," Malao said. He scratched his head. "So what are we going to do now?"

Hok stared at Malao, unblinking. "We're going to stay here and watch Ying."

"*Stay here and watch Ying?*" Malao repeated. "Grandmaster told us to run and then separate. You even agreed that that made the most sense."

"I've changed my mind," Hok replied. "If you disagree, then by all means go. It's probably best if I stay here alone, anyway. You'll just end up talking too much and get us caught."

"Hey, what's that supposed to mean?"

"Nothing," Hok said, shaking his head. "Forget it. Is there anything you want to tell me, Malao? I notice your stick poking out of your robe."

Malao looked down and shoved the decorated

stick back into the folds of his robe. "Oh, yeah. I ran into a soldier who was carrying it. I took it from him."

"You took it from him?"

"Yep. I snatched it away, then I knocked him unconscious."

"So he's still alive?"

"Of course he's still alive," Malao said. "I'm no killer."

Hok's thin eyebrows raised up. "We need to hurry, then."

"Hurry with what?" Malao asked. "I thought we were just going to sit around and watch."

"We are, but first we need to retrieve Grandmaster's body. And we must do it while it's still dark."

Malao twitched. "What? Why?"

"We need to bury Grandmaster and pay our respects."

"P-pay our respects?"

"Yes, otherwise his spirit will never be at rest," Hok said. "Is this a problem for you? Why are you trembling?"

"N-no problem here," Malao replied.

"Good," Hok said as he stood. "Grandmaster's body lies near the main gate. If you can stage some type of diversion, I think I can sneak in and then back out without being noticed."

"That's all you want me to do? Get some soldiers' attention?" Malao took a deep breath and wiped his brow. "That's easy. Do you think those soldiers are superstitious? Because I was thinking, if they're afraid of ghosts—"

Hok frowned. "Don't get carried away, Malao. All we need is a simple distraction."

Malao pouted.

Hok shook his head. "Here's what we'll do. We'll wait until things settle down, then you and I will sneak over to the compound wall that backs up to the bathhouse. Do you remember that tall tree inside the compound where the wall by the bathhouse and the front wall meet?"

"You mean the large elm in the corner?" Malao asked.

"Yes," Hok replied. "You scale the outer wall by the bathhouse and hide in that tree with a handful of rocks. I'm going to sneak around the front wall and hide in the shadow of the gate. When I'm ready, I'll wave my arm, then you toss the rocks onto the bathhouse roof one at a time. Hopefully, that will distract the soldiers long enough for me to grab Grandmaster and slip back out again. If we're lucky, the soldiers won't notice the body is missing until morning."

"I'm not sure rocks will be enough of a distraction," Malao said. A smile began to form on his lips. "What if—"

"Don't push it, Malao. Just toss some rocks and come straight back here. I'm going to do a little eavesdropping now. You sit tight until I return. Got it?"

Malao nodded and casually scratched his upper lip in an effort to hide his uncontrollable grin. He must have been successful because Hok hopped out of the hollow and sailed down from the tree.

CHAPTER 4

Ying stood alone in the moonlight in front of the Cangzhen sleeping quarters. The deep grooves in his face stretched as he yawned. He needed to rest. So far, he had only partially succeeded with his mission. Cangzhen had been destroyed, and proof of Grandmaster's death was on its way to the Emperor. But he didn't have the scrolls, and his five little brothers were still on the loose.

Ying spat on the ground. His brothers' escape was particularly upsetting. He had spent his entire life watching those five get special treatment because of a past none of them knew about. Ying had always guessed the boys held a special place in Grandmaster's heart. And after seeing how far Grandmaster had gone to protect them, he was now sure of it. Since the boys were so important to Grandmaster, Ying decided that they must pay the ultimate price in order to fully repay the blood debt Grandmaster owed him.

Since leaving Cangzhen, Ying had learned many things about his past. But the worst was that his father had been killed by Grandmaster, who had then plucked Ying away from his family. Ying had always had vague memories of this, but he'd been just a toddler at the time. He'd never been able to make out the face of the culprit. However, since he'd learned the truth, those memories had begun resurfacing in the form of nightmares. Nightmares about his father— a powerful dragon-style master—falling to Grandmaster's own dragon-style fists.

Ying was now certain he had dragon blood in his veins. And yet Grandmaster had raised him as an eagle. There could never be worse punishment for Ying or any other warrior monk than being raised as something other than what you truly were. Now that Ying was in a position to judge, he had taken it upon himself to issue the punishments. He had already executed Grandmaster's sentence. Soon it would be time to punish the five young monks.

In the meantime, however, he needed some sleep. Ying entered the sleeping quarters and opened the trapdoor that led down into the Cangzhen escape tunnel. He'd used the tunnel as a back door to launch the attack, but when he'd lived at Cangzhen it had been a peaceful refuge for him. He hoped it could be a sanctuary for him now. He called out to his number two man.

"Commander Woo! Report to the tunnel entrance in the sleeping quarters. Immediately!"

A moment later, the squat, powerful Commander burst into the room carrying a torch. "Sir? Is everything all right?"

"Yes, yes," Ying replied. "I'm just going down into the escape tunnel for a while. I do not want to be disturbed for any reason. I will reactivate the monks' traps down there, so tell the men to stay out."

"I understand, sir," Commander Woo said. "I will spread the word."

"Good. When I come back up, I expect to see additional piles of armor stripped from our fallen soldiers. Order the men to search the compound for bodies one more time, too. I want to review the fallen monks again to double-check that all five boys did indeed escape. It that clear?"

Commander Woo pushed his armor-clad shoulders back and nodded. "Yes, sir!"

Ying grunted and dropped into the pitch-black escape tunnel to try to get some sleep.

"Wake up," a voice whispered in Malao's ear.

Malao opened his eyes and saw Hok's pale face. It glowed in the moonlight spilling in through the hollow tree's entrance.

"Ying has gone down into the escape tunnel and his number one soldier, Tonglong, has left on a mission," Hok said. "It's time to get Grandmaster."

Without another word, Hok drifted out of the hollow. Malao groaned and hurried after him.

As he raced along the ground, Malao struggled to keep up with Hok, who floated effortlessly through the thick underbrush. No matter how many times he saw Hok travel like this, Malao couldn't seem to get used to it. It was just plain unnatural for a human to be able to travel so swiftly and silently through so many obstacles. If anyone could sneak inside Cangzhen and grab Grandmaster's body, it was Hok.

Unfortunately, Hok wasn't very good at planning distractions. Tossing a few rocks might attract the soldiers' attention, but not for very long. Malao had a plan of his own that was much better—not to mention a lot more fun!

Hok stopped behind a large bush at the edge of the tree line and scanned the area with a quick twist of his long, thin neck. Without a sound, he motioned for Malao to follow and glided across the grassy expanse toward the compound's perimeter.

Malao remained next to the bush in the moonlight shadows.

Hok reached the wall and looked back at Malao with a confused look on his face. Malao smiled and waved.

Hok signaled for Malao to join him. Malao signaled Hok to continue on.

Hok shook one finger at Malao, silently scolding him. Malao waved back dramatically, like he was saying goodbye to an old friend.

Hok shook his head, then flattened his supple body against the rough stone of the compound wall. He slowly made his way toward the front corner. As soon as Hok slipped around to the front, Malao sprang into action.

Malao ripped handfuls of long, dry grass from the edge of the tree line and stuffed them into various openings in his robe and pants. He left most of the grass hanging out at odd angles. Next, he tore a thick vine from a nearby tree and used it to tie a large bundle of grass to his head. After folding the bundle down over his face, Malao collected a handful of rocks and raced across the grassy expanse.

Without slowing, Malao leaped at the stone perimeter wall, his legs working like he was climbing a ladder. The wall was as high as two men, but after three long strides Malao's free hand reached the edge of the wide top. He pulled himself onto it and sprang into the large elm tree he and Hok had discussed. He was barely in position when Hok gave the signal to begin the distraction.

Malao lobbed a rock onto the steep tile roof of the bathhouse and it rolled down noisily. Five soldiers were positioned between the bathhouse and the main gate, but none of them reacted. The bathhouse was smoldering, and apparently a strange noise on the rooftop wasn't worth investigating. Malao tossed another rock. Even though it rolled off the rooftop and nearly hit the closest soldier in the head, none of the soldiers paid any attention to it.

Malao was glad he'd come prepared.

With a mighty leap, he vaulted out of the tree and landed on the roof tiles, which, he was surprised to discover, were scorching hot! Malao began to howl and dance about in the shadows of the flickering flames. The long grass poking out of his robe swayed like ripples of energy radiating out from a ghostly spirit.

This time, the soldiers all looked up, then dropped to their knees and dug their foreheads into the dirt.

"I told you we should have buried the dead!" one of the soldiers cried out.

"Y-you were right!" said another. "The spirits have come for us!"

Malao smiled. This was working even better than he'd hoped! He peeked through the bundle of grass covering his face and saw Hok hoist Grandmaster over his shoulder and head out through the main gate.

Malao continued to hop from foot to foot on the hot rooftop, waiting a few moments like Hok had said. He noticed the soldiers' foreheads were still pressed to the ground. He couldn't resist having a little more fun before he ran off. Malao cleared his throat and spoke in his ghastliest voice.

"Repent, soldiers! You must respect the dead! Bury monk and soldier alike before you next sleep. Mention what you've seen here to no one, or I will find you. I will hunt you down and devour your souls! I will seek out your wives and your children, your mothers and your fathers, your brothers and your sisters, your—"

Something warm brushed up against the back of Malao's thighs. He spun around and saw that a clump of grass hanging out the back of his robe had caught fire.

Malao yelped and scrambled back across the roof. When he reached the very edge, he jumped, his arms flailing. He felt a leaf brush against one hand and he clamped down tight, grabbing hold of a thick branch.

His momentum in full swing, he launched himself feetfirst toward the perimeter wall and landed smoothly in the center of the wide top. He jumped down to the ground outside the compound and began to roll before finally stopping to grind his backside into the earth.

His thighs and surrounding region still warm, Malao sprang to his feet and raced toward the tree with the hollow. The fire was out, but a thin trail of smoke followed him like a wriggling tail.

CHAPTER 6

Malao scurried along the massive arms of the elm tree that held the hollow. Pausing outside the entrance, he felt a gentle breeze blow across his backside. He twisted around and around in the moonlight, trying to get a good look at his singed robe.

"Whoa," Malao mumbled. "I'm getting dizzy." He giggled.

"Get in here!" Hok whispered from inside the hollow. "Stop playing around."

Malao stopped spinning and wobbled inside. "Sorry," he said as he plopped down across from Hok. "So what did you think?"

Hok sat perfectly straight with his legs crossed. He

stared at Malao, unblinking. "What did I think of what?"

"My performance back at the compound," Malao said. "Wasn't I great?"

"I don't want to talk about it. You could have gotten us both caught."

"Huh?" Malao said. "We didn't even come close to getting caught! Besides, I tried your idea first, and it didn't work. I needed to do something else. If it wasn't for me—"

Hok raised his hand. "The rocks would have worked just fine, Malao. You should have tried throwing a few more before you pulled your little stunt."

Malao raised one hand, mimicking Hok. "Well, I happen to think you're upset because I didn't do *exactly* what you told me to do. You know how much you like being the boss."

Hok shot Malao a stern look. "That's enough, Malao."

Malao giggled.

"Why don't you go sit outside?" Hok said. "I need a few moments alone to think."

Malao shrugged his shoulders and stood. "Suit yourself. I could use some fresh air, anyway. It's getting a little stuffy in here." He giggled again and turned to leave.

"Don't go too far. I'd hate for you to get *lost,*" Hok teased. "Besides, I still need your help."

Malao turned back. "Help with what?"

"With burying Grandmaster."

Malao twitched. "What? Didn't you already take care of that?"

Hok shook his head. "No. When would I have had time to do it? He's only hidden. I need your help getting him up the tree—"

Malao's eyes widened. "*Tree?* What tree?"

"This tree," Hok said. He tapped the floor of the hollow with his bare foot.

"Y-you want to stick Grandmaster inside this tree? W-why would you do that?"

"Because we don't have the tools or the time to bury Grandmaster in the earth. Inside here, it's just like a tomb. You can think of it as a living pagoda, if you like. Just like the Forgotten Pagoda within the Cangzhen walls. Only in this one, Grandmaster will be part of the cycle of life. As his body returns to its basic elements, he will help feed the tree. He would appreciate that."

"Th-that's kind of . . . d-disgusting," Malao said. He wrapped his arms tightly around himself.

"No, that's life," Hok said. "Are you okay, Malao? You're trembling again."

"I'm f-fine," Malao replied. Beads of sweat began to form on his forehead. "I just need some f-fresh air—"

Hok stood and walked over to Malao. "Why don't you tell me what's bothering you? Are you afraid of Grandmaster's remains?"

"M-maybe," Malao replied. "D-dead bodies make

me n-nervous. And you know how I get when I'm n-nervous."

"There's nothing to be nervous about," Hok said gently. "Death is part of life. It's natural. Just put your emotions aside. You'll be all right."

"P-put my emotions aside?" Malao said. "H-how do I do that?"

"Try a meditation exercise. Remember what Grandmaster always used to say? *You must take control of your thoughts and your emotions, or they will control you.*"

Malao shook his head. "H-how can I meditate at a time like this? B-besides, those exercises never work for me."

"They work wonders if you give them a chance," Hok said. "Cangzhen monks have used them for hundreds of years to separate themselves from their emotions. I'll do one with you, then we'll get Grandmaster. Okay?"

"N-no."

"Why not?"

"N-no, Hok," Malao said. "Please—"

Hok raised both hands. "Okay, okay. I'll tell you what, I'll go get Grandmaster myself, but I'd still like your help getting him up the tree. Why don't you go sit out on a limb until I return. We'll see how you feel when I get back, all right?"

Malao wiped the sweat from his brow with a shaky forearm and nodded.

Hok nodded back and drifted out of the hollow without saying more. He disappeared into the undergrowth.

Malao stepped outside and took a deep breath. The night breeze brought with it the smell of smoke from the Cangzhen compound. Malao began to shiver uncontrollably.

I can't do it, Malao realized. *I just can't.*

He leaped into an adjacent tree. Then another and another. Fueled by nervous energy, Malao raced into the night. When he was tired from jumping tree to tree, he ran. When he was tired from running, he walked. In no time, he was hopelessly lost. Out of breath, his eyes filled with tears, he eventually found himself at the bank of a small stream.

Malao dipped his hands into the cool water and sloshed them around in an effort to relieve his callused palms. It helped some, so he stepped into the stream to cool his bare, aching feet. Extremely thirsty, he bent over to take a long drink, then stuck his face into the flowing water and left it there awhile, soothing his puffy eyes.

After some time, Malao stood and walked upstream until he came to a large willow tree. He climbed into it and nestled himself in a large forked branch, hidden from below by a curtain of newly formed leaves. Exhausted and alone, he drifted off to sleep.

Late the next morning, Malao woke to four eyes staring at him. The eyes blinked, then disappeared behind a wall of willow leaves.

Malao sat up and poked his head through the leaves. He saw two brown macaques racing off through the treetops. A troop of more than one hundred was moving toward the same stream he had waded in before climbing the tree and falling asleep.

After what he had been through, Malao was in no mood to tangle with a monkey troop. Sometimes macaques could be aggressive. Malao hopped to his feet, and a tremendous racket erupted beneath the willow. He looked down and saw three monkeys standing around the base of his tree, scolding him.

Out of the corner of his eye, Malao noticed a fourth monkey approaching. It was pure white and larger than the others. It looked like it might weigh almost as much as Malao did. The white monkey began to pace back and forth on bent legs and straight arms below the willow, its thick thigh muscles and forearms bulging. It barked out orders, and different groups of monkeys responded accordingly. Some drank from the stream, while others kept an eye out for danger.

As Malao stared, the white monkey looked up at him and bared its teeth. Malao saw that it had only one eye. He also saw that it had four razor-sharp fangs, each as long as his thumb. He knew what those were for. Malao grabbed hold of the decorated stick tucked into his robe and began to pull it out.

The white monkey zeroed in on the movement. Its icy eye locked on Malao's. The other monkeys stationed beneath the tree stared, too.

Malao stopped. He knew he usually reacted aggressively to aggressive actions like someone raising a weapon, so he decided to do just the opposite. He slowly removed his hand, leaving the weapon hidden. Then he sat back and did his best to relax.

To Malao's relief, the monkeys below relaxed, too. The white one even stopped pacing. Still, the white monkey and the enforcers remained beneath the tree with their eyes glued to Malao.

Malao scratched his head. The monkeys' behavior confused him. He had never seen a group of macaques as militant as this. And he had certainly never seen monkeys on the ground keeping an eye on a potential enemy in a tree. It was usually the other way around.

The white monkey barked once. At the stream, a group of mothers stepped up to the water's edge with babies clinging to their bodies like large brown clumps of thistledown. Behind the mothers, two young monkeys played roughly. Malao noted how their attacks and defensive maneuvers mirrored the movements he made during his training exercises. Like him, the monkeys' arsenal included an unlimited combination of tumbles, jumps, dodges, sweeps, feints, and strikes.

The young monkeys were both about the same size, and they seemed equally matched. However, Malao knew that most monkey-style kung fu techniques had been developed with the assumption that your opponent would be bigger and stronger than you. These techniques helped him tremendously when fending off his larger, older brothers in both formal sparring matches and everyday roughhousing. To help him close the gap even further, Malao had trained extra hard. He had had to make up for what he lacked in size with quickness, accuracy, and stamina.

Monkey-style kung fu was very demanding, but Malao had pushed through all the pain—often pushing himself until he dropped. Literally. One of the most grueling exercises he performed was called Monkey Rope training. It was designed to develop strong back and shoulder muscles, which are critical for the swinging movements central to monkey-style kung fu. Malao would climb a thick rope hanging from the top of Cangzhen's tallest tree, using only his hands. He would then climb down again, still using only his hands. And then he'd climb back up. And then back down. Over and over until his hands bled.

To make matters worse, Grandmaster would sometimes stand on the ground at the end of the rope, watching. After Malao made ten or eleven trips up and down the rope, Grandmaster would begin to swing the rope wildly in an attempt to throw Malao off. Grandmaster was usually successful. Malao would fly through the air, frantically grabbing at tree branches as he tumbled back to earth. Fortunately for Malao, he always managed to grab hold of something with his aching hands before it was too late.

Still, Malao had always felt that Grandmaster would have somehow managed to catch him if he had ever plummeted to earth. As strange as it sounded, Malao knew part of him would miss Grandmaster always pushing his skills to their limits.

Downstream, the farthest group of monkeys began to chatter frantically. Their mood swing was contagious. The rest of the groups screeched and shrieked in succession before racing downstream to join the mayhem. With the white monkey in the lead, the group of enforcers below Malao's willow raced off, too.

In the distance, Malao heard a voice cry out, "MONKEYS! MAN THE CARTS!"

Chapter 8

Malao scurried through the treetops to see what the commotion was all about. Long before he actually saw anything, he heard cries from both monkeys and men. When the scene finally came into view, Malao's heart sank. A massacre was unfolding.

The monkeys were swarming down from the trees onto large carts that rested on a wide trail. Thirty or forty men surrounded the carts in small groups. The men waited until a cart was completely covered with monkeys before drawing their weapons and lashing out. Quick and agile, most of the monkeys managed to escape the swinging swords and stabbing spears. However, some of the younger monkeys fell to the weapons.

To Malao's disbelief, monkeys continued to pour out of the trees, back onto the same carts. Malao assumed the monkeys were determined to get their hands on anything edible, regardless of the risk. Oddly, most of the carts didn't seem to contain food. When the monkeys lifted back the heavy blankets covering the carts, Malao saw gold. Huge piles of gold.

Malao shivered. He had seen enough death at Cangzhen to last a lifetime. He needed to stop the slaughter, but it would be no easy task. The men protecting the gold were extremely skilled with their weapons.

"Look what I got!" one man shouted as he hoisted a speared monkey high overhead. "Lunch! For all my friends!"

The men roared with laughter.

"Hey, I got one, too," another man called out. "Seven or eight more and we'll have a feast!"

The group cheered.

"Watch the gold!" a third man shouted. "I just speared one trying to make off with some. Don't they realize that *we're* the bandits in this region? No one steals from us!"

"Here, here!" the group chanted, and Malao realized the bandits were enjoying this. It was a game to them. A cruel, deadly, horrible game. They didn't have to kill the monkeys. All they had to do was shoo them away. That's what the monks did if they were transporting items and encountered a monkey troop in the forest.

"STOP!" Malao yelled. He burst through the treetops and landed on top of one of the gold carts.

The bandits stared at Malao, surprised. The monkeys, however, continued to leap onto the carts.

The monkeys must really be desperate for food, Malao thought. *Or gold. But what would monkeys do with gold?*

Several monkeys began grabbing gold bullion from the cart Malao was standing on. The bandits immediately resumed their assault.

Malao took action. He jumped and waved his arms, and monkeys scattered. He twisted and scurried and swiped, and monkeys leaped off the carts. Determined to continue until every last monkey left the area, Malao flipped and kicked and swayed and swung and leaped from cart to cart, and soon a tremendous shrill filled the forest from high up. The monkeys immediately abandoned the carts and returned to the trees.

Breathing heavily, Malao looked into a tall oak tree and saw the large snow-white monkey scowling down at him with its one good eye.

"What did you do that for?" one of the bandits sneered at Malao. In his hands was a bloody spear.

Malao spun around and glared at the bandit from atop a gold cart. He crouched low, ready to spring. His hands trembled.

A second bandit, holding a broadsword, approached Malao. "A better question for our little friend is, *Just who do you think you are, meddling in our business?* Are you some kind of animal-loving monk? I notice you're wearing an orange robe. You've got to be the tiniest monk I've ever seen."

Malao bared his teeth and began to shake violently. Out of the corner of his eye he saw a huge, hairy man approaching empty-handed. The man was one of the largest humans Malao had ever seen. His face was covered by a heavy black beard and his forearms were blanketed with hair as thick as the greasy mass on top of his head. Extremely tall and large-boned, the man cast a shadow over every bandit he passed. His enormous stomach jiggled and sloshed with every step.

The giant spoke with a deep, thunderous growl. "Quiet! I will handle this. Answer the questions, boy. *Why did you do that,* and *who do you think you are?*"

Malao pulled himself tight into a ball in an effort to control his shaking. His teeth rattled as he spoke. "I—I did that because it is not necessary to kill the monkeys. All you have to do is shoo them away. As for my name, it is Malao."

A few of the bandits laughed. The large man questioning Malao remained dead serious. "Why would you call yourself *Monkey*? And why did you choose a Cantonese word for your name? Are you from Canton?"

"I did not n-name myself," Malao replied. "The Grandmaster of our temple did. He was Cantonese. Our temple was not in Canton, though. It was in this v-very region."

· "And what temple would that be?" the burly man asked.

"It was called C-Cangzhen Temple," Malao said. "But you would never have heard of it. It was s-secret."

"Why do you talk about it in past tense?"

Malao trembled. "It was d-destroyed last night."

The big man paused and his close-set eyes narrowed. He stared at Malao that way for quite some time, as if waiting for Malao to say something. Malao felt like he was about to burst from the tension of the moment.

"Why did you kill those monkeys?!" Malao shouted suddenly. "What did they ever do to you?"

The large man's nostrils flared. "What business is it of yours?"

"Where I come from people don't kill animals," Malao said. "Especially monkeys!"

"Well, where I come from, boy, we do kill animals—especially monkeys. We eat them. And we enjoy it very much. Why should that concern you?"

"People get along fine without eating meat," Malao said. "Just look at me. We were allowed to eat meat at our temple for special occasions, but I've never eaten any. Ever!"

A grin spread across the large man's face. "Oh, I believe you. Perhaps if you ate some meat, you wouldn't be so small."

Malao frowned and the bandits laughed.

The big man seemed to relax. "Let me see if I understand you. You would like me to stop eating monkeys, even though I've been doing it my entire life. Is that what you're saying?"

"Yes," Malao replied.

"Well then," the man asked in a polite tone. "Do you have any more requests, young man?"

Malao stood up, his anxiety slipping away. "Well, since you asked, me and my brothers are supposed to uncover the secrets of our pasts. We are orphans. Maybe you could help."

The big man smirked. "You mean you want me to help you find your parents? Or maybe a long-lost uncle?"

Malao shrugged. "I guess that's what it means."

"Isn't that sweet?" the large man said, smiling now. "Your temple was destroyed, and now you want Mommy and Daddy to help you seek revenge."

Malao stared at the man. He suddenly had a feeling he was being toyed with.

The big man turned to the bandits and bellowed, "Gentlemen! Monkey Boy here says he's searching for his family. It looks to me like he found them. Don't you agree? I believe that is his sister stuck like a pig at the end of that spear!" The large man pointed to a spear held by one of the bandits. The spear-holder raised the spear high and shook it. The bandits roared with laughter.

Malao began to shiver again.

One of the bandits shouted, "Hey, I wonder if his father is the Monkey King? The kid really seems to enjoy hanging out on top of that gold cart!"

The bandits roared again.

Malao felt a powerful jolt behind his eyes as if he'd been blindsided by a roundhouse kick.

"*Monkey King?*" he mumbled. That name sounded familiar to him. Of course, he knew about the monkey king of legend—a magical creature that supposedly lived thousands of years ago. However, Malao was almost certain the bandit was referring to a real person. Someone who simply had the nickname Monkey King. Malao shook his head to clear his senses.

"Aw, stop teasing the boy," another bandit yelled out. "You know there's no Monkey King. The monkeys only steal gold because it's shiny and they like to look at it. They don't deliver it to anyone. Leave the boy be and let's get on our way."

"This boy isn't going anywhere," the big man replied, suddenly serious. "He's robbed us of a feast. He belongs to me now. My stomach has been aching for days because I haven't had any fresh meat, but I know a cure. Liver soup. I've made it before with monkey livers, and it worked wonders every time. However, they say it works best with human liver!"

The huge man lunged at Malao. Malao leaped straight into the air. He touched down on top of the man's greasy head and bounded toward the trunk of the nearest tree. Malao latched on to the tree for the briefest of moments, then sprang in a completely different direction an instant before the big man slammed his shoulder into the tree. The tree shook violently and the entire group of bandits erupted with laughter. The large man winced.

Malao looked down from high atop a large maple. He saw the big man pull a small object from one of several pouches hanging from his sash. It was a throwing dart! The man's eyes seemed to drift apart and Malao focused on the one eye that remained on him, prepared to leap if the man launched the dart in his direction.

The large man's hand suddenly flashed outward in a blur, but not in Malao's direction. It followed the path of the drifting eye. High atop a neighboring tree, the white monkey cried out. It fell to the ground, clutching its head, and the big man pounced on it.

Malao howled and leaped down from the treetop, landing in the center of the large man's back. He grabbed the short, greasy hair on the back of the man's head with his left hand and yanked the decorated stick from his robe with his right. As Malao raised the stick, one of the man's enormous hands flew back and grabbed it. The man swung his huge arm powerfully down. Malao let go of the man's hair and grabbed on to the stick with both hands as his body was flung forward over the man's shoulder.

Still holding on to the stick, Malao landed flat on his back next to the white monkey. He groaned.

Upon seeing the stick, the monkey seemed to lose its mind. With one paw against its bleeding head, it unfurled its other claw and slashed viciously across the top of the large man's hand. The man cried out and let go of the stick. The monkey bared its long, razor-sharp fangs and launched its face at Malao's hands. Malao let go as the monkey clamped its jaws down onto the stick.

The white monkey sprang to its feet, the stick in its teeth, and darted off into the trees. Malao leaped after it but fell heavily to the earth as a large net was cast over him. Several men held the ends of the net down, out of Malao's reach. Malao wriggled and clawed and kicked, but it was no use. He stopped struggling and stared up at his captors through the tightly woven holes in the net.

The burly man walked away, only to return moments later carrying a huge pair of golden melon hammers. The large, round heads of the war hammers glistened at the end of metal handles, each as long as Malao's leg. The big man stared coldly at Malao as he raised his huge arms in preparation for a crushing blow.

"That's very brave of you, Hung—killing a child with the aid of several others and a net," a voice called out from the crowd. "I speak a little Cantonese myself, you know, and I recognize your name as Cantonese, just like the boy's. How strange. Cantonese names are so rare in this region. Stranger still is the significance of your name. *Hung* means 'bear' in Cantonese, and you really do remind me of a bear. A big, lazy panda bear. If you were a *real* man, you would dismiss your helpers and fight the boy alone, hand to hand."

Malao knew that voice. It belonged to his brother Seh!

CHAPTER 9

Outside the Cangzhen perimeter wall, Commander Woo squinted in the late-morning sun and ran his fingers through a section of charred earth. He raised one hand to his nose, and his head recoiled from the smell. "Are you certain this mark was left by a ghost?" he asked the soldier beside him.

"Yes, sir," the soldier replied nervously. "I'm positive. I believe it is the same restless spirit we've felt watching us. It may also be the same one responsible for stealing the Grandmaster's body. Last night, four other soldiers and I saw the spirit soar from the burning rooftop right through the middle of the tree behind us. It touched down on top of the wall and paused before floating down somewhere beyond, which I believe is right where we're standing now. Flames followed it the whole way down. I think that's what burned the ground here. It must be a very powerful spirit to have fire flowing from it like that. I'm concerned, sir."

"Concerned about what?" Commander Woo asked.

The soldier lowered his head and shuffled his feet. "The spirit promised to hunt me and the others down and devour our souls if we mentioned what we saw to anyone. It said it would go after our families, too—"

"What's this nonsense about a spirit?" Ying suddenly appeared from around the front corner of the perimeter wall.

Commander Woo jumped. "Sir!"

"Don't you remember our little discussion earlier this morning, Commander?" Ying asked. "I thought I made it clear that I didn't want to hear any more talk of spirits. Now I find you out here, *still* discussing spirits. Why are you indulging the men with this nonsense? Ghosts do not exist."

Commander Woo cleared his throat and pointed to the ground. "But we have proof, sir."

"Step aside," Ying said. He stuck his face near the burn mark. The grooves in his face deepened as he grimaced. "I know this smell. One of the young monks has made it a habit to skip as many bathing sessions as possible. His feet are particularly pungent." Ying looked at the soldier. "Tell me what you saw last night. Or at least what you *thought* you saw."

The soldier cleared his throat. "Pardon me for saying this, sir, but I saw a spirit. I am certain of it. What I saw could not have possibly been a human, let alone a boy."

"Why do you say that?" Ying asked.

"The spirit leaped all the way from the bathhouse roof, through the middle of that large tree, to the wall behind us. It landed perfectly in the center of the wall and paused for only the briefest of moments before floating down to the ground beyond. No human could do that."

"Do you think a monkey could do it?" Ying asked.

"Well, I don't know . . . ," the soldier said, rubbing his chin. "I suppose. But monkeys can't talk, sir. The spirit we saw gave us a warning."

"Listen closely, soldier," Ying said. "You listen, too, Commander Woo. Share this information with the other men. I have reviewed the bodies of the fallen monks a second time, and I am certain five boys escaped our attack. One of the boys is called *Malao,* which means 'monkey' in Cantonese. I believe he is the one who took the decorated stick from that useless soldier on the night of the attack. He is probably still around. Malao could make the leap you claim is impossible for a human. I've seen him do more impressive things in the past."

"But, sir," Commander Woo said. "Surely any human that could manage a leap like that is in some way connected to the spirit world."

Ying snickered. "No, Commander. You are mistaken. At times these boys seem superhuman, but believe me, they are not. They are just very, very skilled and have extraordinary natural abilities. Fortunately, not all of them have learned to control their instinctive behaviors. This makes them vulnerable. We shall catch them, and you will see for yourself. But that is still several days off."

"Several days, sir?" Commander Woo asked.

"Maybe more, maybe less," Ying replied. "Who knows with this pathetic group of soldiers. Tonglong is on his way to the Emperor, and Captain Yue and his men are out searching for the boy called Fu, who stole the dragon scrolls from us. I don't expect either of them to return for a couple days, and we will not make any major moves until they both return. Do I make myself clear, Commander?"

Commander Woo swallowed hard and nodded.

CHAPTER 10

"Fight! Fight! Fight!" the bandits chanted. Secured in the net, Malao struggled to catch a glimpse of his brother Seh among the bandits. It took Malao a moment to recognize his tallest brother, who stood at the front of the group wearing a brilliant blue silk robe. Seh's long, narrow eyes were barely visible beneath a fine silk hat that covered his bald head. He looked much older in that outfit.

The bandit Hung pointed one of his enormous war hammers at Seh. "Why don't *you* fight him, newcomer?"

"I have no complaints against the boy," Seh replied. "In fact, if it were up to me, I would let him go. I thought he performed valiantly. But out of respect for your grudge, I suggest you fight him. We form a ring, and the two of you battle until only one is left standing. The one standing determines the fate of the fallen one. What do you say, *Bear*? Or are you afraid of the little monkey?"

"Watch your mouth," Hung warned, "or your liver may end up in my soup, too. I don't care that the men have already welcomed you into our group. You've only been with us a few hours. You've yet to prove yourself in my eyes. I will gladly—"

"HUNG!" said a deep voice from the back of the group. Malao watched as the bandits parted and a second giant of a man came forward. While Hung was one of the largest humans Malao had ever seen, this man was *the* largest. And Malao had seen him before. The giant had occasionally been a guest of Grandmaster's at Cangzhen!

The man was impossible to forget. He wore a red silk robe as big as a tent, and his head and face were smooth like a monk's. In fact, every speck of the man's glistening skin was strangely devoid of hair. He didn't even have eyebrows. Like Hung, the bandit leader was extraordinarily tall and big-boned. Unlike Hung, this man was pure muscle. The sleeves of his robe bulged and rippled as he folded his gargantuan arms and addressed Hung.

"What are you up to now?"

"I'm just about to tenderize my lunch," Hung replied, waving a hammer. "Would you like to join me, Mong?"

Mong? Malao thought. *That's another Cantonese name! It means "python." That man kind of looks like a python, just like Hung kind of looks like a bear. What's going on here?*

"You're going to eat that little boy?" Mong asked, chuckling. "He wouldn't even qualify as a snack for you, big man. Let him go, and let me get back to business."

Hung growled. "I don't think so, boss." He held up his bleeding hand. "This happened because of him."

Mong laughed. "Is that why everyone was chanting, 'Fight, fight, fight'? Because you got a little scratch on your overgrown paw?"

Hung snarled, and one of the bandits spoke up. "The newcomer suggested a fight to settle the score, boss. Let's let them fight! I want to wager. I'll take the monkey boy, along with all the money from anyone who wants to bet on Hung!"

Malao watched as several bandits rushed toward the man who'd spoken. There was a flurry of fast-talking. Gold coins exchanged hands. Mong grinned and walked over to Seh. "Well, I guess we've got ourselves some afternoon entertainment. Would you care to wager, newcomer? Since you're the one who suggested the fight, I'm presuming you'll take the boy."

"I don't have any money," Seh replied. "But if I did, I would bet it all on the boy."

Mong smiled and slapped Seh on the back. The bandit leader reached into the folds of his robe and removed a sizable pouch. He held it high over his head and announced, "I bet this entire bag of gold on the boy! Somebody give him a weapon and let the games begin!"

The bandits cheered and Hung grunted. Malao watched Hung take several steps back as the net was lifted and the bandits formed a circle around him and Hung. Hung twisted and stretched with his huge hammers in hand, preparing for battle. Malao stood weaponless.

"Didn't you men hear me?" Mong said to the group. "Somebody give the boy a weapon!"

No one responded.

Seh looked firmly at a bandit holding a long, tasseled spear. Even from a distance, Malao could tell the spear was well made. The tassel was perfectly positioned at the bottom of the metal spearhead where the spearhead connected to the wooden shaft. The main purpose of the tassel, made of long brown horsehair, was to distract an opponent from the spearhead's razor-sharp tip. Its secondary purpose was to absorb any blood that might run down the shaft, making the weapon slippery for the user. Apparently this particular tassel was effective. It glistened red with fresh blood.

Seh approached the bandit. "Let the boy borrow your monkey skewer."

"I don't think so," the bandit replied. He gripped the weapon with both hands and raised it over his head, out of Seh's reach. "I wagered on Hung and—"

Seh's long arms suddenly lashed out in a flash of blue silk. Malao saw him extend the first two fingers on each hand and strike both of the bandit's arms high on the inner biceps, near the man's armpits. The bandit's arms instantly slumped to his sides, limp. The spear dropped to the ground.

Malao glanced at Mong. Mong was grinning.

"Thanks," Seh said to the bandit. He relaxed his snake-head fists, picked up the spear, and hurled it at Malao.

Malao dropped to the ground and rolled sideways, thrusting his right arm straight up into the air. When he felt the tassel brush against his hand, he clenched his fist, catching the spear halfway down the shaft. He completed his roll and sprang to his feet.

Malao switched the spear to his left hand and brought his right hand up to his nose. He sniffed the blood that had been painted across it by the flying tassel. His upper lip curled back as he turned to face Hung.

Hung roared and raced toward Malao, his hammers raised high. Malao knew that the best defense against a war hammer was to not be there when it struck, so when the hammers came down, he leaped to one side.

There was an explosion of dirt as the hammers plowed matching craters into the earth. When the dust cleared, Malao was far from the damage. He stood in the exact center of the bandit ring, waiting.

Hung growled and lifted his hammers high once more. This time, he walked slowly toward Malao.

Malao straightened his arms and held the spear

out before him with both hands, parallel to the ground. But instead of placing his hands shoulder-width apart like most spear users, he placed his hands side by side at the spear's center balance point. He crouched low and bent his elbows, bringing his arms in to his sides. He relaxed his wrists and his hands sagged. The spear hung loosely in his curled fingers. Malao looked exactly like a monkey that had paused while eating an extraordinarily long piece of fruit.

Laughter erupted from the ring of bandits.

"Look at him!" one of the men shouted. "That's hilarious!"

Even Hung grinned. He stopped two steps from Malao's shivering body and lowered one hammer to adjust the pouches hanging from his sash. He raised the hammer again.

"P-please, I don't want to hurt you," Malao said. Nervous energy raced through his system. His teeth rattled.

The bandits around Malao burst into laughter again. Hung's grin disappeared and he took an enormous breath. As Hung exhaled, he brought the hammers down a second time.

Malao let out a terrifying screech and spun powerfully to his right, narrowly avoiding one of the heavy hammerheads. As he turned, he tucked one end of the spear under his right arm, locking it firmly in place with his elbow. Still in a low crouch with one full revolution nearly complete, Malao lunged toward his opponent.

The swinging spear shaft connected with Hung's lead ankle. Hung howled in pain and tumbled to the ground face-first. Malao released the spear and sprang onto the enormous man. One of Malao's thighs landed on each side of Hung's head.

Hung roared and stood awkwardly as Malao locked his legs around Hung's neck from behind. Malao began to pound Hung's temples with fierce, open-palm strikes.

With another tremendous roar, Hung dropped the hammers and reached back, grabbing Malao's robe with both hands. Hung struggled to rip Malao from around his neck, but Malao's powerful legs held firm. Hung began to swing his gigantic fists, and Malao knew he had to think of something fast. He took a deep breath, straightened both his index fingers, and jammed them as hard as he could into Hung's ears.

Hung screamed and the ring of bandits widened as every man winced and took several steps back. Hung grabbed hold of Malao's wrists and yanked so hard that Malao had to let go with his legs or risk having his arms ripped out of their sockets. Caught off guard by Malao's sudden release, Hung stumbled forward and let go of Malao in order to catch himself before his face hit the dirt a second time.

Malao flew forward and tucked into a tight series of rolls. When he finally stopped, he spun around and saw Hung with his hammers in hand, trying to stand again on his one good leg.

Malao launched himself at that leg.

Hung hopped backward using one hammer as a cane. He raised the other hammer high and bellowed like a bloodthirsty beast. Malao landed short of Hung's good leg and threw himself forward onto one shoulder as Hung swung the raised hammer. When Malao felt the earth against his shoulder blade, he kicked straight up into the air with both legs.

Hung's mighty blow stopped in midair as both of Malao's feet connected with Hung's groin. Hung's eyes crossed and he teetered for a moment before crumpling to the ground, immobilized. Malao barely had time to roll out of the way.

Malao stood and backed away from Hung. Covered head to toe with dust and sweat, Malao looked over at Seh. Seh winked.

Mong laughed and stepped forward into the ring with Malao.

"Well done, little one!" Mong said. "To date, I'm the only one who's been able to put Hung in his place. It seems I must thank you for earning me a handsome sum from my friendly wagering with the men. You were a long shot, you know."

Malao shrugged. Mong reached out as if to lay a hand on Malao's shoulder and Malao took several steps back.

Mong laughed. "There's no need to be nervous. At least not until Hung can see straight again." Mong paused and rubbed his shiny, hairless head. "Speaking of Hung, I believe you have earned the right to do what you will with the big oaf. Are you in the mood for liver soup?"

Several of the bandits gasped. One of them cried out, "You're not really going to let the boy kill Hung, are you, boss?"

"In all honesty," Mong replied, "I hope the boy doesn't kill Hung, but it is his right. A deal is a deal. We may be bandits, but we're honorable bandits. We keep our word." Mong looked at Malao. "So, what's it going to be, boy?"

Hung lifted his face from the dirt and glared at Malao, his eyes still crossed.

Malao's face hardened. He walked over to Hung and spoke in a shaky voice. "Roll over."

Hung shook his head.

Mong sighed and walked over to Malao's side. He swung one enormous leg back and kicked Hung hard in the ribs with his heavy boot. "The one who defeated you fair and square said *roll over*. Do it. Now."

Hung groaned and rolled over. Malao grabbed one of the pouches hanging from Hung's sash. He opened it, peeked inside, and threw it to the ground. Then he grabbed another, and another, throwing each to the ground after opening it. Malao peeked inside the next pouch and grinned. He tied the pouch to his own sash and turned to Mong.

"I will leave Hung his life and take this prize instead," Malao said in his best grown-up voice.

Mong smiled. "Thank you, little one."

Malao lowered his head and shrugged.

Mong knelt down to Malao's height. "I suggest you leave the area immediately, my little friend. I don't think I'll be able to stop Hung once his eyes straighten out."

Malao looked at Mong and nodded. Mong nodded back.

Without a word, Malao leaped onto the nearest branch and headed for the treetops. He looked back to wave goodbye to Seh, but all he saw was a flash of blue silk.

The sun was still high in the sky when Malao stopped next to the stream and climbed down from the tree-tops. He squatted and cupped some cool water in his aching hands.

As he drank, Malao thought about Seh and the bandits. He hoped Seh knew what he was getting himself into. That was a rough bunch. Mong didn't seem too bad, though.

Malao scratched his head. *How many times have I seen Mong at Cangzhen?* he wondered. *Four? Five?*

Malao remembered that Mong had always come alone, but that didn't make his visits any more justified. After all, he was a bandit. A very successful bandit.

Malao couldn't believe how much gold the bandits

had. He couldn't imagine where they got it, let alone what they might do with it. Even though monks weren't supposed to have an interest in material things, Malao had never been able to keep his eyes off anything made of the precious metal. It hypnotized him. Several of the pouches Hung carried had been filled with gold, and Malao had had a hard time throwing them aside. He didn't know why, but he felt he should take only one pouch from Hung, and it should be something useful.

Malao untied the pouch from his sash and sat down on the stream bank. He dumped out the contents. There was a loud *CLINK!* and a brief spark as a firestone and a metal strike bar collided on the firm earth. Gold was nice to look at, but these items would be a lot more comforting on chilly evenings. More important, he could use them to start a fire for cooking. That is, if he ever managed to find something to cook.

Malao rubbed his stomach. He was hungry.

What can I eat? he wondered. There wasn't going to be any fruit for many more months, and plants were just beginning to poke up through the soil. Monkeys ate things like tree buds this time of year, but that wouldn't work for him.

Frustrated, Malao stood and kicked a small pile of leaves beneath a large tree. His toes dug into something soft and slimy. He grinned.

Lunch! Malao thought. He leaned over and carefully pushed the leaves aside. His heart leaped as he uncovered a cluster of mushrooms.

All Cangzhen monks learned which plants and

fruits were safe to eat, and mushrooms were no exception. Some types of mushrooms could make you sick or sleepy. Others were lethal. Great care was taken to make sure only the safe ones were served at the Cangzhen dining table. Malao was often recruited to scour the forest floor in search of mushrooms. He was confident these were not only safe, they were delicious.

In a flurry of leaves and flying dirt, Malao picked several handfuls and set them aside. Then he rounded up enough dry twigs and tinder to start a small fire with his new firestone. Once the fire was going, he found two long sticks about as big around as his little finger and carried them to the stream, along with the mushrooms.

Malao dunked the long sticks in the stream. He would use them as roasting skewers, and he didn't want them to burn. Sticks freshly broken off a living tree would have been better because they wouldn't burn as easily, but he didn't see a need to damage a perfectly good tree just to make his life a little easier.

When the sticks were sufficiently wet, Malao stuck one end of each in the bank and began separating the large mushroom caps from their stems. He rinsed each cap in the stream before sliding it onto a skewer. The stems he tossed into the flowing current.

In no time, the mushrooms were roasting over the open flames, filling the air with an irresistible aroma. So irresistible, in fact, that Malao soon found he had a visitor. The white monkey.

Malao saw the monkey high in a nearby tree. It was

staring at him with its single eye. A clump of matted hair and dried blood was stuck to one side of its head.

Malao did his best to ignore the creature, but it kept staring. He knew monkeys normally ate mushrooms, so he assumed it was hungry. It was probably in pain, too. When Malao was down to his last two mushroom caps, he spoke to the monkey.

"Would you like some?" Malao asked. He stepped away from the fire and held out the stick. To his surprise, the white monkey scurried down from the tree and cautiously approached him.

Malao stood perfectly still, his arm outstretched. He had seen firsthand what kind of damage the monkey could do when it wanted to take a stick from someone.

The monkey gently took the far end of the long mushroom skewer and slowly pulled it from Malao's hand. Malao expected the monkey to race off into the trees, but it didn't. It sat down and began to eat the remaining mushrooms.

Unsure of what to do next, Malao just stood there. When the white monkey finished, it politely handed the skewer back to Malao. Malao couldn't believe it.

He had an even harder time believing what happened next.

The white monkey moved closer to him and rose up on its hind legs, its right hand extended. Malao reached out, too, and the monkey grabbed his hand. The monkey pulled Malao's hand to its nose and took a deep breath.

Malao kept his eyes fixed on the monkey's mouth. He knew what lay behind those lips. The monkey's mouth began to part, and Malao fought the urge to yank his hand away. Something deep inside him told him to leave his hand right where it was. He was glad he did.

The white monkey planted a kiss on the back of Malao's hand, then released it and raced back up into the tree. A moment later, the monkey returned with the decorated stick from Cangzhen in its teeth. It dropped the weapon at Malao's feet and scurried off into the treetops.

Night had settled in, and Malao found himself still on the ground near the stream. He was too tired to try to locate a suitable tree to spend the night in, so he curled up at the base of a small willow. The low-hanging branches made him feel safer. He'd waited and waited for the white monkey to return, but it hadn't. He was disappointed. He thought he had made a new friend.

Malao began to wonder what it would be like to go through life without any friends. He decided it might be a lot like going through life without any family. What a horrible thought.

Malao twitched. He suddenly realized *he* might go through life without family or friends. After all, he was completely on his own now. Grandmaster was dead and his four brothers were scattered without any sort of plan to get back together.

What if something happened to me right now? Malao wondered. *Would anyone ever know? Would anyone even care?*

A story drifted into Malao's mind. A tale from the famous Shaolin Temple, whose former members had founded Cangzhen Temple more than a thousand years earlier.

The monks at Shaolin had a long history of building pagodas to honor the remains of people important to them. It is said there was a special pagoda at Shaolin much smaller than the rest, built to honor a small boy. Legend had it the boy was helping the cook one day, but he failed to show up for the evening meal. During dinner one of the monks found a strange bone in his soup, and the monks realized what had happened. The boy had fallen into the enormous pot they used to cook the soup. The monks were so upset they built a pagoda to honor the boy.

Malao used to think that was the funniest story he had ever heard, and he used to retell it all the time. But none of his brothers ever laughed. He was beginning to understand why.

Something else Malao used to joke about no longer seemed funny. It was the Forgotten Pagoda, which was located within the Cangzhen walls near the front of the compound. Malao used to think it was hilarious that somebody had taken the time and energy to build it hundreds and hundreds of years ago but today no one remembered who was buried inside it. That wasn't funny, Malao now realized. That was sad.

I should have helped Hok bury Grandmaster in the tree, Malao thought. *A living pagoda—that's what Hok had called it.*

Tears welled up in Malao's eyes. He had never mourned anyone before because he'd always snuck away from the few burials that had taken place at Cangzhen while he was growing up. He decided it was time he learned how to mourn someone. After all, who would bother to mourn him if he didn't care enough to mourn anyone else?

Maybe Hok could help me? Malao thought. *Unless...* Malao shook his head. *Unless I offended him so much that he doesn't want me around anymore.*

Malao began to shiver uncontrollably. Inside his head, it seemed like he was sliding down a steep, muddy slope in the middle of a thunderstorm. No matter how hard he tried, he couldn't make it back to the top. He just kept slipping down, down, down. All he could think about was the family he didn't have—

Or don't have yet? he realized.

The rain began to slow in Malao's head. He remembered what the bandit Hung had said about finding his parents or maybe an uncle. Hung had been joking, but what if it were true? What if he did have some family members alive somewhere?

Malao took a deep, cleansing breath, and his shaking subsided. The prospect of new family members was exciting, but he still missed his old family. Even though his brothers picked on him a lot, they would always stick up for him when things turned bad. Just like Seh had done. Malao thought it might be nice to join Seh, but he knew that was impossible after what had just happened with Hung.

I'll go back and join Hok then, Malao decided. *I'll apologize, and maybe he'll understand. That is, if I can find the way back to Cangzhen. . . .* Malao shook his head. *Why didn't I pay closer attention when I ran off?*

Malao felt thunderclouds begin to roll inside his head again. He closed his eyes and did his best to clear his mind with one of the meditation exercises Grandmaster had taught him, just like Hok had suggested. It took some time, but he eventually managed to push everything out except a single question that had been in his head much of the day. A question that somehow still made him think about family.

Who was the man called Monkey King?

He just couldn't remember.

Malao yawned. At least he had managed to sweep most of the clutter from his head. He was beginning to understand why the older monks enjoyed meditating so much. It was very relaxing. With his mind almost empty, sleep soon overtook him.

As usual, Malao's night was filled with vivid dreams. Dreams of slippery slopes and monkey kings. Dreams of pagodas and soup pots.

And a particularly vivid dream about a large snake slithering over him, coiling itself tightly around his body as it swallowed his face.

CHAPTER
12

Malao woke in the dark, barely able to move, barely able to breathe. A firm hand covered his mouth and nose, and his arms were pinned to his sides. He twisted and turned and kicked and bit—but it was no use. His opponent always seemed to be one step ahead of him.

When Malao realized this, he gave in a little. To his surprise, so did his opponent. The hand squeezing his face seemed to soften more and more as he struggled less and less.

"Easy, little brother," a voice hissed in his ear.

Malao let his body go limp and the blanket of pressure around him released. The hand slipped away from his face, dragging a trail of snot across his cheek.

"That's disgusting!" Seh said as he climbed off

Malao in the darkness. He wiped his hand on Malao's shoulder. "Don't you ever blow your nose?"

Malao giggled and sniffed loudly. He wiped his face on the sleeve of his orange robe. "That's what you get for smothering me in my sleep, you sneaky snake. How did you find me?"

"I saw mushroom stems flowing down the stream earlier," Seh said. "I thought they might be from you, so I walked upstream. Sorry I didn't come sooner. I had to wait until dark before I snuck out."

Malao rubbed his eyes. "What are you doing here?"

"I came to check on you," Seh said, slinking to the ground. "That was some fight you had with Hung. He moaned and groaned the rest of the day from the beating you gave him."

"He deserved it," Malao said.

"Of course he did," Seh replied. "I had to beat several bandits senseless myself before the gang stopped attacking me. I didn't even do anything to provoke them." Seh paused and looked off into the darkness. "Did you hear something?"

"No," Malao said. He rubbed his bald head and stretched. "Why would you want to join a gang of bandits?"

"I'm hoping to earn their trust so that maybe they'll help us. They're very powerful, you know."

"They're *bandits*, Seh. Why would they help us?"

"They aren't ordinary bandits. I think with a little time—" Seh stopped and stared off into the darkness again. "Did you hear that?"

"No," Malao said. "I didn't hear a thing. And I don't believe you came out here just to check on me. I know how sneaky you are. What are you *really* up to?"

"Listen, I can't talk long," Seh said. "Do you have any news for me? Tell me, quick."

Malao paused and blinked several times. "Grandmaster is dead."

"What?" Seh whipped his head around to face Malao. "Are you sure?"

"Yes," Malao replied. "I helped Hok retrieve the body."

"Hok! Where did you see Hok?"

"At Cangzhen."

"But Hok was the one who pushed hardest for us to run and then separate," Seh said.

"I know," Malao said. "Hok really surprised me when he snuck up on me while I was spying on Ying."

"You returned to spy on Ying?" Seh asked. "That's pretty bold, little brother."

Malao smiled. "Yes, it is. But not as bold as what Fu did. He swiped the dragon scrolls."

"What?" Seh said. "I can't believe I missed all this. Fu? Are you sure? Ying said that he sent his number one man to get those scrolls. You mean to tell me that that overgrown pussycat defeated Ying's number one soldier?"

"I guess so," Malao said.

"Amazing," Seh said. "I didn't know Fu had it in him. Did you or Hok happen to see Long?"

"No," Malao replied.

"Me neither." Seh paused. "So is Hok . . . okay?"

"Yeah, Hok is fine. Why?"

"No reason," Seh said, looking sideways. "What are you going to do next?"

"I was going to try to find my way back to Cangzhen and see how Hok is doing. Do you want to come with me?"

"Well . . . no. I'm going to stay with the bandits and . . ." Seh's voice trailed off. He listened, then shook his head. "Look, Malao, I've got to get back."

"Wait," Malao said. "Do you know why some of the bandits have Cantonese names? I mean, doesn't that seem strange to you? And what's going on with their leader, Mong? I know I saw him with Grand-master at Cangzhen several times."

Seh looked sideways again. "I have no idea what you're talking about, Malao. Now, I really need to—"

A twig snapped and Malao sat up straight. He glanced around but didn't see anything. He looked over at Seh.

Seh was staring in the direction of the sound. After a moment, he whispered, "I need to get out of here, Malao. I don't sense anyone, but I can't take any chances. Good luck, little brother."

Malao opened his mouth to say something, but Seh had already slipped away into the night.

Malao shrugged his shoulders and curled up beneath the small willow tree. He closed his eyes to welcome sleep again and grinned as he thought about Seh's exit. Seh was always so dramatic.

Hidden in the thick underbrush several paces from Malao, Mong also grinned. He, too, turned and slipped away into the night.

CHAPTER 13

Malao woke the next morning when the sun began to warm the willow leaves above him, sending heavy drops of dew cascading onto his forehead. He wiped his brow and walked to the stream for a quick drink, then built a small fire and scoured the area for more mushrooms. It didn't take him long to find some. It took him even less time to prepare them. Soon the heavenly aroma of roasting mushrooms filled the air.

To Malao's surprise, the white monkey appeared again. But instead of lurking in the treetops, this time it came down and sat right next to him beside the fire. The monkey scratched the large scab on the side of its head. Malao winced.

The monkey winced, too, mimicking Malao. Then it crossed its legs and sat up straight, just like Malao. It looked at Malao with its one good eye as if waiting for a reaction.

Malao laughed and handed the white monkey one of the two long skewers he had prepared. He expected the monkey to gobble down the half-cooked breakfast, but the monkey held the stick out and continued roasting the mushrooms over the flames, just like Malao was doing.

Malao grinned and the monkey seemed to grin back. The monkey scooted closer to Malao. Malao and his new friend sat that way long after they had finished cooking and eating.

"Well, my friend," Malao finally said to the white monkey, "I've got to get going. You can come with me if you'd like. Unfortunately, I don't know how long I'll be gone because I can't remember how to get there."

The monkey looked at Malao, concern written across its face.

Malao laughed. "Don't worry, I'll be fine. Too bad you can't show me the way to Cangzhen."

Upon hearing the word *Cangzhen,* the white monkey began to jump up and down, chattering excitedly. It pointed into the trees.

"You can't be serious," Malao said. "Do you really know the way?"

The monkey stopped jumping and cocked its head to one side. It looked confused.

Malao grinned. "I knew it. You don't understand me, do you?"

The monkey continued to stare at Malao as if waiting for something.

Malao sighed. "I thought so. I'll never find my way back to Cangzhen."

Once again, the white monkey got excited. This time, it grabbed Malao's hand, squeezed three times, and raced off into the trees.

Malao shrugged and followed.

Malao ran for what seemed like forever. He had long since stopped trying to keep up with the white monkey in the treetops. Instead, he traveled on foot as the monkey tirelessly raced from tree to tree. Malao's neck grew sore from looking up.

By early evening, the terrain began to look familiar. Malao climbed up to the monkey's side, and they traversed the treetops together. From that point on, Malao led.

They stumbled upon the large hollow elm sooner than Malao expected. When they were still some distance away, Malao took cover behind the trunk of a large oak, just in case. The monkey curled itself into a tight ball next to him.

A moment later, Malao realized hiding wasn't necessary. He could feel Hok's intense gaze burrowing through the trunk, seeking him out. Malao climbed around to the front of the oak. There was Hok, poking his head out of the hollow and staring directly at the spot where Malao was hiding. Malao waved.

Hok leaped from his perch and glided through the treetops. He landed next to Malao.

"I was afraid you wouldn't return," Hok said. "I owe you an apology. I shouldn't have pushed you to do something you weren't ready to do. I'm sorry."

Malao lowered his head. "There's no need for you to apologize. *I'm* the one who should apologize for running off like that."

Hok reached out and raised Malao's chin with a pale finger. "Don't worry about it, little brother. Are you feeling okay? You don't look so good."

"I'm fine," Malao said. "Just a little tired. And a little sad, I guess." He looked over at the hollow. "Where is Grandmaster?"

"He's in the tree," Hok replied.

"You got him up there yourself?"

Hok nodded.

"But there aren't any stains on the trunk or the ground or anything."

"I was very careful," Hok said. "Would you like to see what I did inside?"

"Um . . . I . . ." Malao's voice trailed off. He closed his eyes and took a deep breath. "Yes. Yes, I would like to see."

"Good," Hok said. He patted Malao on the shoulder. "You can bring your little friend, too, if you want."

The white monkey poked its head out from behind the trunk and looked at Malao. Malao shrugged.

Hok grinned and launched himself toward the hollow. Malao and the white monkey followed. Once inside, Malao looked around.

"It looks exactly like it did the last time I was in here," Malao said.

"Yes," Hok replied. "I found a small hole in the floor and widened it. There's an enormous cavity beneath us that seems to run the entire length of the trunk. That's where Grandmaster now lies. As you can see, I plugged the hole thoroughly. No one will ever know he's in there."

"You've been busy," Malao said. "It looks great. I'm sure Grandmaster appreciates it."

Hok's brown eyes sparkled. "Thank you, Malao. But now that it's done, I'm sure he'd like us to focus on Ying."

"Yeah," Malao agreed. He glanced outside and saw a green tree snake slithering up a tree trunk. "Hey, I need to tell you about Seh!"

"Seh? What about him?"

"I saw him," Malao said. "Twice, actually."

"This better not be a joke, Malao."

"It's not a joke. He joined a gang of bandits."

"I'm sorry, did you just say *bandits*?"

Malao grinned. "Yes, but Seh said they're not ordinary bandits."

"I don't understand," Hok said. "What kind of bandits are they?"

"Who knows?" Malao replied. "We're talking about Seh, remember? You know how he is."

Hok rubbed the back of his long, thin neck. "Do you know if Seh happened to cross paths with Long?"

"He said he hadn't. I wonder where Long disappeared to?"

"I haven't the slightest idea," Hok said. "I—"

Hok froze in mid-sentence. He glanced around the hollow, then lowered his voice. "I'd like to hear more about your adventures, Malao, but I think we should keep our talking to a minimum. I have a feeling someone is nearby."

The white monkey scurried over to the hollow's entrance and peeked out.

Malao began to fidget. He whispered, "Since we need to stay quiet, why don't you show me how to do it now?"

"Do what?" Hok asked.

"You know," Malao said, shuffling his feet. "Do what we came in here to do. Pay respects to Grandmaster."

"You've never paid respects to someone?"

Malao shook his head.

"You never cease to amaze me, Malao," Hok said, shaking his head. "Let's make this quick. Grandmaster is basically below us, so just lower your head and do as I tell you."

Malao took a deep breath and nodded. He was a little worried he might do something wrong and offend Grandmaster's spirit, but he figured he would probably offend Grandmaster's spirit more if he didn't try at all.

"Close your eyes," Hok whispered in a peaceful tone. "Fold your hands in prayer and bow three times slowly while thinking of something you would like Grandmaster to hear."

"What should I think of?" Malao asked.

"That's up to you," Hok said.

"Well, what did *you* tell him?"

"That's between me and him. Now don't talk, just think. And listen with your mind. You might be surprised by what you hear."

Malao concentrated. *I'm sorry if I offended you, Grandmaster. I now realize I should have helped Hok bury you.*

Malao waited for a response. He didn't get one. He tried again. *And I'm sorry I thought burying you in a tree was a disgusting idea.*

Still no response. Malao focused as hard as he could, struggling to think of something else. *I'm also sorry I used to joke about the Forgotten Pagoda.*

For a moment, Malao swore he heard a voice. A familiar voice. He concentrated harder. *And I won't ever joke about the boy in the soup again!*

This time, Malao was sure he heard something. He opened his eyes wide. "Hey, Hok, did you hear—"

"Hush," Hok whispered.

Malao slammed his eyes shut and reached out once more with his mind. His heart began to race as he imagined Grandmaster's spirit trying to communicate with him.

His heart nearly stopped when he realized the voice he was hearing wasn't Grandmaster's. It was Ying's.

CHAPTER 14

"Get over here, Commander Woo," Ying said in a harsh whisper. "Our prey is near. I can feel it."

Ying scanned the ground. He didn't see any tracks in the dirt, but that didn't mean anything. He knew his quarry often spent time in the trees.

"Yes, sir!" Commander Woo said as he approached, his chest puffed out.

"Quiet," Ying hissed. "I don't want to give our target a head start by announcing our presence. Keep your voice down."

Commander Woo's shoulders slumped, and he nodded.

Ying opened the large leather bag he had slung over one shoulder and began to dig around. "Before we continue, Commander, I have a question for you. Your family name—*Woo*—means 'witchcraft' in Mandarin, does it not?"

"Yes, sir," Commander Woo replied. "That is one translation."

"Do you or any of your family members practice the black arts?"

"No, sir. Not that I'm aware of. Why do you ask?"

"Because you are so superstitious," Ying said. "Also, because some call what you are about to see witchcraft. I thought you might be familiar with the procedure."

Ying removed a small green pouch from the leather bag. He handed it to Commander Woo.

"Open it. Carefully."

Commander Woo's large hands fumbled with the drawstrings on the slippery silk pouch. He peeked inside.

"Do you know what that is?" Ying asked.

"It appears to be some kind of powder, sir. Though I can't identify it."

"It's powdered dragon bone," Ying said. "There is a secret place where men pull the bones from black liquid earth under the light of the full moon. They grind the bones to make this. It is very, very expensive. A thousand times more than its weight in gold. So be careful when you carry it."

Commander Woo raised his eyebrows.

"You are responsible for that pouch now," Ying said. "Along with everything else in this leather bag. I am going to show you how to make a special elixir. From this day forward you will prepare it for me every evening. Doing so will serve two purposes. First, it will help you overcome your fear of the spirit world. Some claim the preparation of this drink attracts hungry ghosts who want a taste, but you will see firsthand that this is nonsense. No spirits will bother you, because spirits do not exist. The second purpose is perhaps more important. I find myself spending far too much time searching for a key ingredient every evening. You will now find it as part of the preparations."

"If you don't mind my asking, sir," Commander Woo said, "what is the ingredient?"

"Blood," Ying replied. "But not just any blood—a very specific kind. And it must be fresh."

Commander Woo swallowed hard. "Dare I ask what this potion does for those who drink it?"

Ying smiled. "Let's just say it brings me closer to my kindred spirits." He lurched forward, baring his pointed teeth and flicking out his forked tongue with a hiss. Commander Woo jumped.

Ying laughed. "Relax, Commander. I'm just toying with you. Now, I want you to—"

Ying stopped in mid-sentence. Every muscle in his body seized in an act of total concentration. He sensed something moving. Something specific. He leaped high into the air and thrust a powerful eagle claw around the tree next to him. When he hit the ground, a green tree snake writhed in his iron grip. Ying looked at Commander Woo.

Commander Woo backed away.

"Get over here," Ying said.

"But that snake is poisonous, sir!" Commander Woo said. "I can tell by the shape of its head. Be careful."

Ying scowled. "I know it's poisonous, Commander. That's the point. It has to be a poisonous variety for the elixir to be effective. I'm holding it firmly behind its head. It won't bite you—unless I release it down your collar."

"S-sorry, sir," Commander Woo said as he walked briskly to Ying's side.

With his free hand, Ying removed a small ornate goblet from the leather bag and handed it to Commander Woo.

"Hold this cup in one hand," Ying said, "and hold the pouch open in the other."

Commander Woo did as he was told. Ying dipped a long fingernail into the powder and scooped up a small amount. He dumped it into the goblet.

"You will use a small spoon for measuring," Ying said. "I will show it to you another time. At the moment I seem to have my hands full." He grinned and grabbed the snake by the tail with his free hand. He unwound the snake from his wrist and found it to be nearly as long as his arm.

"This is a good length," Ying said. "Now, hold that cup perfectly still, Commander. Don't you dare move."

Ying placed the snake's tail between his sharp teeth and clamped down hard. Waves of pure muscle rippled through the snake as it struggled to free itself.

Ying lifted the snake's head high into the air and leaned toward Commander Woo. Commander Woo flinched but held the goblet steady.

Ying positioned his face over the goblet and thrust a razor-sharp fingernail into the underside of the snake. Blood poured down its belly into the goblet. After a moment, Ying hurled the snake into the underbrush. He smiled a wide, toothy grin.

Commander Woo grimaced.

Ying laughed and took the cup. He began to stir the blood and dragon bone mixture with one of his long fingernails. "Do you think you can handle that, Commander? I'm guessing *you'll* use a knife, though."

Commander Woo took a deep breath and nodded. "Yes, sir."

"Good. I will expect you to bring me one each evening no later than one hour after sunset."

Ying licked his lips with his long, forked tongue and raised the goblet. He closed his eyes and drank slowly, savoring every drop.

CHAPTER 15

It was the middle of the night when Malao felt someone shake him gently.

"Wake up," Hok whispered. "We need to talk."

Malao sat up and rubbed the sleep from his eyes. "What's going on?" he mumbled. He looked around the hollow and saw the white monkey sitting in one moonlit corner.

"You fell asleep again," Hok said.

"I did? When?"

"Hours ago."

"Is everything okay?"

"No," Hok replied. "I went out and did a little reconnaissance. There's something you need to know."

"Don't even tell me Ying is catching more animals," Malao said. "What he did to that snake earlier was disgusting."

Hok closed his eyes. "What I have to tell you has nothing to do with Ying. It has to do with Fu. He's been captured."

"WHAT?" Malao said.

"Hush," Hok said. "Do you want us to get captured, too?"

"Sorry," Malao whispered. "Where is he?"

"He's in a village less than a day's travel from here. Ying's number one man, Tonglong, has returned, and I overheard him and Ying talking about it. Ying has sent his number three, Captain Yue, and fifty soldiers to collect Fu from the villagers."

"Let's go," Malao said. "We probably don't have much time."

Hok shook his head. "We can't. I'd like to help Fu, too, but we don't even know where the village is located. We have to wait until we know more."

"Wait?" Malao said. "What more do we need to know? Fu is in trouble! He's our brother, and we have to help him!"

"Keep your voice down," Hok said. "I know it's difficult to accept, but there's nothing we can do. Not only does Captain Yue have fifty men, Ying also sent Commander Woo with a large group of reinforcements to meet up with them. Even if we could find the village, we wouldn't have a chance."

"You're always so . . . logical," Malao said, frustrated. He took several deep breaths. "What if we got to the village before Captain Yue?"

"You'd have to find it first."

"Maybe my friend here can show us the way. He led me back to Cangzhen." Malao looked at the white monkey. The monkey came over to his side and sat down.

Malao scratched his head. "What's the name of the village?"

"I don't know," Hok replied. "All I know is the Governor lives there and—"

The white monkey suddenly jumped up and grabbed Malao's hand.

"Hey!" Malao whispered. "He knows the word *Governor*! I bet he knows where the village is! Let's go!"

Hok raised one hand. "Even if your little friend is clever enough to find the village, I think at least one of us should stay here to keep an eye on Ying. There is much at stake, Malao."

"I know what you're saying, but I have to do something, Hok. Fu is part of our family."

Hok stared at Malao, unblinking. "If you don't get to Fu before Captain Yue does, Fu will be surrounded by at least fifty soldiers. Do you understand what you'd be getting yourself into?"

"Not really," Malao said. "But that's never stopped me before." He grinned.

Hok sighed. "If you feel you must go, I understand."

Malao nodded. He squeezed the white monkey's hand three times and released it. The monkey sprang into the darkness.

Malao waved goodbye to Hok and shot out of the hollow like a lead ball from a *qiang*.

The rest of the night, Malao followed the white monkey through the forest. By sunrise, they reached the spot where he had slept near the stream. The white monkey let out a long shriek and the entire monkey troop came into view.

To Malao's surprise, the white monkey leaped onto his shoulder and released a tremendous howl. Every monkey in the troop took notice. The white monkey patted Malao's bald head, howled again, and raced upstream. The rest of the monkeys followed. So did Malao.

The monkeys didn't pay much attention to Malao, and Malao gave them even less notice. He was too busy trying to follow without losing his footing on the slippery stream bank. It got even worse in the middle of the day, when they changed directions and turned into the forest. Unable to pick his way through the thick undergrowth, Malao took to the trees. In no time, his hands began to ache and his shoulders grew sore. He knew he couldn't keep this up much longer. Fortunately, he didn't have to.

In the distance, one of the monkey scouts began to chatter. The rest of the troop instantly reacted, screeching and howling and carrying on like they had when they encountered the bandits' caravan.

A voice rang out through the forest.

"ON YOUR GUARD! MONKEY TROOP! PRO-TECT THE SUPPLY CARTS!"

Great, Malao thought. *Here we go again. . . .*

CHAPTER 16

Ying looked up from the trail as the sound of screeching macaques and shouting soldiers filled the forest ahead. He turned around to face Tonglong, who was riding high atop his stallion. The horse's pitch-black coat glistened in the midday sun.

"Do you recognize any of those voices?" Ying asked.

"Yes," Tonglong said. "Some of the voices belong to Commander Woo's unit, and some belong to the soldiers you sent with Captain Yue. The two groups must have rendezvoused."

"I agree," Ying said. "It's a good thing we left Cangzhen when we did. It sounds like a monkey troop is getting the best of them. I believe I heard Captain

Yue shriek like a woman a moment ago." Ying shook his head. "I had a hunch those two would somehow botch this assignment. Stay here while I investigate. When your unit catches up, have them prepare their *qiang*s. Perhaps we'll have monkey stew tonight."

"What do you intend to do?" Tonglong asked.

"I'm not sure," Ying replied. "But whatever it is, you can bet it will be something . . . educational." He smirked.

Tonglong shifted in his saddle.

Two soldiers carrying a long pole approached from behind Tonglong. A pale young monk in an orange robe hung from the pole, bound at the wrists and ankles like a hunting trophy. The monk appeared to be unconscious.

"Here comes your unit now," Ying said. "Make sure the entire group is assembled before you move forward. In the meantime, remain as quiet as possible and keep an eye on Hok. You should take as much care restraining him as you did catching him last night. Though he's a crane, he can be as sneaky as a snake."

"*He*, sir?" Tonglong asked.

Ying's eyebrows raised and the furrows in his forehead deepened. "Well, well. I see you've discovered Hok's little secret," Ying said softly. "I'm impressed. Not too many people know. I only found out after I left Cangzhen. Do me a favor and keep this tidbit to yourself. It's bad enough the men know Hok successfully spied on us the past few days. Their confidence might be further shaken if they knew how hard you had to work to catch a girl."

"As you wish, sir," Tonglong replied.

Ying nodded and disappeared up the trail. He soon heard the unmistakable rustle of men racing across the forest floor. The shrieking of the macaques was growing closer and more urgent.

Ying stepped off the trail.

A moment later, a single soldier ran down the trail toward Ying as though his life depended on the speed of his feet. The man spent more time looking back over his shoulder than he did looking forward on the trail. This was unacceptable behavior for a soldier—especially one within Ying's ranks.

I said I would teach the men a lesson, Ying thought. *Class is now in session.*

Ying locked one arm around the trunk of a tree to anchor himself and thrust his other arm out in front of the fleeing soldier's neck. The soldier's eyes bulged in surprise as his head snapped back and his feet flew out from under him. Ying was on top of the man before he even hit the ground.

"Where do you think you're going?" Ying hissed in the man's face. His forked tongue flickered.

The soldier choked several times before mumbling, "Monkeys, sir . . . the monkeys have gone mad."

Ying looked up and saw a number of screeching macaques fanning outward through the treetops.

"You're armed soldiers!" Ying said. "What's wrong with you?"

"They attacked us, sir. They're chasing us down. I swear I've never seen anything like it."

"Where are Commander Woo and Captain Yue? Have they run off, too?"

"I don't think so, sir. Captain Yue is in his sedan chair and Commander Woo is inside a . . . aahhh . . . weapons cart."

"What?" Ying said. "They're *hiding*?"

"These are not normal monkeys, sir," the soldier said. "They seem to be organized and led by a human— a small, dark child monk who carries a white monkey on his shoulder. Some of our men attacked the boy as he tried to release another child monk called Fu from a cage we—"

"Fu!" Ying interrupted. "He's up ahead?"

The soldier nodded.

"What about the scrolls?"

"I think Fu may have them by now, sir."

"Fu got out of the cage?"

"Yes," the soldier replied. "The other monk threw him a ring of keys and—"

"ARRRGH!" Ying leaped off the soldier and soared into the nearest tree. From there he could see into a small clearing farther up the trail and, sure enough, there stood Malao and Fu, talking. Fu seemed confused and upset. Malao, as usual, appeared to be making jokes. There wasn't a single soldier around.

Ying spat and sailed to the ground. He worked his way silently through the underbrush, stopping when he reached a large bush directly behind Malao. As

Malao continued his banter with Fu on the opposite side, Ying slid his chain whip out from one of his over-sized sleeves. In one lightning-fast motion, he wound up and lashed out around the side of the bush at ankle-height. Ying heard the familiar *whoosh!* and a satisfying *clink! clink! clink!* Even more satisfying was the sound of air rapidly exiting Malao's lungs as Ying yanked on the chain and Malao slammed into the dirt.

"Come here, you little knuckle-dragger!" Ying snarled as he stepped through the bush and pulled Malao toward him. Both Malao's ankles were wrapped tightly together with one end of the chain whip.

Ying looked over at Fu, and Fu's mouth dropped open. Ying was amused to see the scabbed-over slice in Fu's cheek stretch to a point where it had to hurt. Ying glanced down at Fu's chest and saw a dragon scroll poking out. He was about to lunge for the scroll when he noticed Fu's body go rigid.

Ying turned and saw Tonglong approaching with his men. Near the front of the group was Hok hanging from the pole.

"FU! HELP ME!" Malao cried.

Ying smirked as Fu leaped next to Malao and grabbed the end of the chain near Malao's feet. Fu's robe opened slightly and Ying saw more scrolls. As he prepared to launch himself at Fu, Ying heard monkeys approaching. Angry monkeys. He looked up and saw dozens of macaques racing toward him through the treetops.

"Fire!" Ying commanded, and shots rang out from

the *qiang*s carried by Tonglong's men. Monkeys rained down around them. A piercing screech filled the air, and Ying noticed a white monkey run off into the trees. Blood dripped from its arm. The remaining monkeys followed the white one's hasty retreat.

Ying laughed. "Fine fighting force you have there, Malao."

Fu growled and said, "Finer than the men you lost at Cangzhen! At least most of the monkeys . . . *GRRRRR* . . . escaped . . . *ARRRRR* . . . alive!"

Through the taut chain, Ying felt Fu tense in preparation for a mighty jerk. Ying chuckled to himself. The instant he felt Fu's big pull begin, Ying let go of the chain.

Fu sailed backward and Ying soared forward toward his closest opponent—Malao.

"Don't let him grab you!" Fu cried out.

But it was already too late. Ying clamped down on Malao's exposed neck with a powerful eagle claw. His razor-sharp fingernails pierced Malao's skin, sinking deep into a pressure point. Ying grinned at Fu as he squeezed, his nails slicing into Malao's nervous system like thin, ragged knives. Malao slipped into unconsciousness.

Ying watched Fu's eyes fill with fury. Ying discreetly formed an eagle claw with his free hand and took a deep breath. An instant later, Fu leaped at Ying's outstretched arm, attempting to break Ying's grip on Malao.

Fu can be so predictable, Ying thought. As Fu

smashed into his arm, Ying released Malao and lashed out with his other hand, latching on to the back of Fu's neck with amazing speed. Fu didn't have a chance. Like Malao, Fu was unconscious within moments.

Ying lessened his grip on Fu and removed the scrolls from Fu's robe. He addressed his men.

"Did all of you see that?" Ying said. "That is how you take care of business! Quickly, efficiently, decisively!"

Ying glanced over at one of the weapons carts and saw Commander Woo sitting inside it with the hatch open. The Commander's right leg was bent at an odd angle.

"COMMANDER WOO!" Ying said. He pointed to Hok. "Look what Tonglong has caught. There is your restless spirit from Cangzhen, hanging from that pole. He was the one you felt watching you, and he snatched the Grandmaster's body from beneath your nose. Hobble over there on your one good leg and untie the one called Hok so that he can walk. He's going on a little trip."

Commander Woo nodded and Ying looked over at Captain Yue's sedan chair. The silk curtains were drawn tight.

"CAPTAIN YUE!" Ying shouted. "Get yourself out from behind those curtains this instant." Captain Yue poked his head out and Ying continued. "You will tie up the two troublemakers known as Fu and Malao, and they, too, will walk. Their paralysis is only temporary, so I suggest you hurry."

Captain Yue made a sour face but nodded in consent. Ying scowled and turned to Tonglong.

"TONGLONG! You have proven your loyalty to me by capturing Hok. Now it is time for you to get your hands dirty. You will finish what was left unfinished back at the temple. Kill these monks. We will set up camp here for the night, so make sure you take them far into the forest before completing the job. I don't want any tigers coming around here to dine on their corpses or lap up their blood. If you run into any problems, fire a warning shot from a *qiang*. I'd hate to have to interrupt my reading to clean up any mess you might make, so don't make any mistakes. And make sure you pay special attention to Fu. He's already gotten away from you once."

"I give you my word," Tonglong said with a gleam in his eye. "I'll take care of the one called Fu."

"We'll see about that," Ying replied. "Don't forget to keep an eye on Hok. And keep a tight leash on Malao, too. Malao may not look like much, but he's a tricky little runt. Now get out of here!"

CHAPTER 17

Very little time had passed, but Ying knew his world had changed forever. As he lay on his sleeping mat inside his tent, he rode a wave of emotions he had never known. He tried his best to relax, but nothing seemed to work. He was just too excited.

Now I know how Malao feels most of the time, Ying joked with himself. *Pity I'll never get to tell him.*

Ying was immersed in reading the first dragon scroll. His brain absorbed the information like a thirsty sea sponge. For the first time ever, Ying felt a connection with something. It wasn't a person or a place, it was a philosophy—an approach to life outlined within the first dragon scroll. He had always assumed the secret scrolls for each animal kung fu style contained advanced fighting techniques—and they did—but they also contained other things: mental guidelines, spiritual guidelines, and much, much more.

Back at Cangzhen, Ying had always been criticized for focusing all his energy on the martial aspects of his eagle-style training. He had ignored the mental and spiritual components, but he had had good reason—the fighting component was the only part that had ever made sense to him.

But now that he was reading the first dragon scroll, Ying was beginning to understand that there was more to kung fu than fighting. Having the nonfighting elements explained in a manner that his inner dragon could comprehend made all the difference. In fact, even the eagle-style fighting techniques he had perfected over time didn't make as much sense as the fighting philosophies described in the first dragon scroll. Ying now saw why dragon-style kung fu was considered the most powerful.

A dragon stylist's life was to be a rich combination of all things: positive and negative, internal and external, hard and soft. At the very surface was the self-defense component, which took the best attributes of the most effective animal kung fu styles known. Dragon-style kung fu involved the use of pressure-point attacks and joint locks from the eagle-style arsenal, pinpoint strikes from the crane style, heavy-handed blows from the tiger style, and circular evasion movements from the snake style, all combined with the unpredictability of the monkey style.

Beyond the fighting techniques, Ying saw another side of martial training he never knew existed: leadership skills. He had had no idea that some people considered leadership an art. The first scroll outlined numerous psychological techniques that could be used to convince men to do what you wanted them to do. There was even a section on psychological warfare.

Ying could feel his power increasing with every line he read. He was more certain than ever that he was born to be a dragon. Strangely enough, some of the psychological techniques Ying read in the scroll were techniques he recognized Tonglong used when directing soldiers. Ying decided to pay closer attention to Tonglong.

Ying closed his eyes. Once his brothers were out of the picture, he would accept the title of General and become the youngest leader ever to report directly to an emperor. While that was an admirable goal, he wanted more. Both his father and Grandmaster had been dragons to the core, but Ying wanted more power than either of them had had. The dragon scrolls would help him first become like them—then surpass them.

A distant *KAA-BOOM!* suddenly cut through Ying's head like a battle-ax through a winter melon.

"ARRRGH!" Ying shouted as he rolled up the first dragon scroll and dropped it onto his sleeping mat. It seemed his visions of greatness would have to wait. His men had just failed. Again. That was a warning shot from a *qiang*.

Ying bolted out of his tent and raced over to Tonglong's horse. He passed a wide-eyed soldier and hissed, "I'll return shortly. Tell the men not to do anything stupid while I'm gone."

Ying unhitched the horse, leaped onto its bare back, and grabbed hold of the reins. He thrust his long toenails into the horse's sides and hung on tight with his powerful thighs, steering the animal as best he could toward the trail Tonglong's men had hacked into the forest.

Horseback riding was not a skill practiced at Cangzhen, and Ying had had little time to learn it while employed by the Emperor. He had a difficult time, to say the least. Branches tugged at his silk robe and pants, and the horse seemed to go out of its way to lean toward any tree limb that might knock Ying and his toenails from its back. By the time Ying reached the clearing where three men lay sprawled on the ground, his clothes were in tatters and his arms and legs were badly scratched and bruised. But he didn't notice. He was too busy trying to make sense of what he saw before him.

All three men lay facedown, spread quite some distance apart. Two of the men were soldiers. The third, with his thick braid and straight sword, was Tonglong. Tonglong and one of the soldiers didn't have any visible injuries, but the third man was a mess. His back appeared to have been shredded by a metal rake. Next to that soldier was a *qiang,* and in front of the *qiang* was a tree with a fresh hole at the base. The soldier must have fired the warning shot. As Ying dismounted, the man-gled man turned his head to one side and moaned. Ying walked over to him and bent down.

"What happened here?" Ying asked in a firm tone. "Who did this to you?"

"A tiger, sir," the soldier replied in a hoarse whisper.

"*A tiger?*" Ying said. "Are you sure?"

The man nodded ever so slightly. "A young tiger came out of nowhere to aid the boy called Fu, just like the monkeys helped the one called Malao earlier."

Ying's carved face darkened. "Where are the boys?"

"Gone, sir."

Ying paused. "Weren't there more men with you?"

"Yes. . . . There were five of us."

"What happened to the other two men?"

"Gone, sir. Chased off by the tiger."

Ying pointed to Tonglong and the other soldier in the clearing. "Are those two still alive?"

"I think so . . . ," the soldier muttered, ". . . just knocked unconscious by the boys. Those boys are not . . . normal, sir."

"You don't have to tell *me* that," Ying snarled. "How long have the boys been loose?"

"I'm not sure, sir. I keep passing out. But I think they ran off as soon as I fired the *qiang*."

Ying looked up at the sun. "By the time we wake those two up and get back to camp, it will be late. There seems to be no point in trying to search for the boys after nightfall. You men can't even seem to get things done in the daylight."

"I'm sorry, sir."

"You should be."

"No, sir," the soldier said. "You don't understand. . . . I'm sorry because I can't answer any more questions. . . . I'm going to sleep now. . . ."

With that, the man closed his eyes and began to snore.

Ying shook his head. For the first time ever, one of his men had done exactly what he said he was going to do.

Ying spat and walked over to Tonglong.

Tonglong appeared to be unconscious. He lay on his stomach, with no identifiable wounds on his back. Ying rolled Tonglong over. The only injury Ying could find was a large lump on Tonglong's forehead, over his left temple. Ying scowled. He knew firsthand that Fu and Malao both had foreheads like iron and could wield them like weapons.

As Ying stared at the lump, his frustration grew. To him, the lump was a symbol of his men's continued failure. The lump pulsed in time with Tonglong's heartbeat, a pink beacon reminding Ying that his future had just taken another step backward.

Ying bent one arm sharply and drove his elbow into the lump. Tonglong's entire body spasmed, then relaxed.

Ying grabbed Tonglong by his thick ponytail braid and dragged him toward the horse, ignoring the two remaining soldiers. He was determined to make it back to camp before sunset.

CHAPTER 18

"Come on," Malao said. "We need to keep moving while it's still daylight."

"No," Fu replied, sucking wind. He plopped down on the forest floor. "I need a break. I don't care if Ying and his men catch up. My legs are killing me."

Malao rolled his eyes and walked over to Fu's side. He sat down and adjusted his singed robe. The decorated stick poked him in the ribs, but he didn't mind. He was just happy Captain Yue hadn't searched him before tying him up.

Malao scratched his head. "Where do you think we are?"

"Still pretty close to Ying's camp," Fu replied. "I can smell them cooking dinner."

"Dinner?" Malao said. "I'm starving. What are they cooking?"

Fu sighed. "Does it really matter? It's not like we're going to get any. I'd rather not talk about food right now."

Malao began to fidget. "Okay, let's talk about something else, then. How about Hok? He didn't look so good back there."

"Hok's fine. You know how tough he is. He's probably just exhausted. Who knows what he went through with Tonglong."

"I guess you're right," Malao said. He scratched his head again. "Do you think what Hok overheard about Grandmaster killing Ying's father is true?"

"I don't know what to think anymore," Fu grumbled.

"What about the other things Hok said? Like Cangzhen being a base for secret activities and Grandmaster being some kind of powerful leader?"

"I said, *I don't know what to think,* Malao. Now will you please be quiet?"

"Fine," Malao said. He stood and stretched. "You know, I can't believe Hok went to Shaolin Temple without us."

Fu growled and stared at Malao. "Why are you still talking?"

Malao folded his arms and pouted.

"You could have gone with Hok, you know," Fu said. "No one forced you to stay here."

"But I felt bad for you, Pussycat. You looked so

lonely back there. I didn't want you to start crying or anything."

"Watch it," Fu said.

Malao giggled. "So what are we going to do about the scrolls?"

"I don't know. I'll think of something. Now, would you mind keeping your rice hole closed? I need to think in peace."

Malao turned away. "Have it your way," he said with a huff. He walked over to the base of a large elm and sprang up onto the lowest branch. As he scanned the tree looking for a suitable resting spot, the scent of cooking drifted past his nose.

Mmmm, Malao thought. *It smells like mushroom soup.* His eyes suddenly widened and he leaped down from the tree, crashing into Fu.

"What the—" Fu began to say.

"Mushrooms! Mushrooms! Mushrooms!" Malao chanted. "Fu, do you think you can take me to the trail Tonglong's men cut through the forest?"

"Probably. Why?"

"I've got a plan, that's why! And it's a good one! Come on, Pussycat, we need to hurry. We've only got until sunset!"

"You look ridiculous," Fu said.

"Do you have any better ideas?" Malao asked.

Fu didn't respond.

Malao smirked. "That's what I thought. Now keep quiet. Ying and his men may come along any moment."

Malao adjusted the clumps of grass poking out of his sleeves and tightened the large bundle tied to his head. He walked over to a cluster of mushrooms and smiled. Just as he suspected—sleeping mushrooms. He'd recognized them when they'd passed by earlier with Tonglong and the soldiers. Malao picked two handfuls and tied them up in the lower corner of his robe. Now all he needed was Ying's pouch of powdered dragon bone to set his plan in motion.

"Let's go," Malao whispered. He crept silently through the evening shadows toward Ying's camp, staying close to the makeshift trail that had led them into the forest with Tonglong. Fu followed, but Malao noticed he looked uneasy. A moment later, Fu signaled to Malao that he heard someone up ahead. Malao motioned for Fu to follow him up a large oak tree. Fu did so without comment. Malao grinned. He was enjoying being the boss for once.

Malao settled into the tree's enormous arms and crossed his legs. He formed a makeshift table on his lap with his robe and untied the knot around the mushrooms. Carefully, he laid each one upside down on his lap and removed the stems. He picked up a mushroom cap and flipped it over into his cupped palm, running a finger across the gills. Tiny spores sprinkled into his hand. He grabbed another cap, and then another, until he had collected spores from all of them.

Malao closed his fist tightly around the spores and stood, brushing the mushroom caps and stems to the ground. They bounced noisily off the large, crunchy leaves that littered the forest floor beneath the oak.

Fu stuck his head around the tree trunk and glared at Malao. "Shhh! I think—" Fu stopped in mid-sentence and snapped his head back around to his side of the tree.

Malao peeked around the tree and squinted into the setting sun. He saw a stocky soldier hobbling in their direction. The soldier had a splint on one leg and carried a large leather bag over one shoulder. He also carried a long forked stick. Malao recognized the soldier as Commander Woo, the man who had held the goblet for Ying when he'd seen Ying bleed a snake.

Malao nodded to Fu. Fu returned the nod and hunched over, preparing to pounce.

But Commander Woo never looked up. He took a quick look around the base of the tree, then limped off into the forest.

Fu looked at Malao. Malao shrugged.

"It's better that he didn't see us," Malao whispered as he folded the bundle of grass down over his face. "Trust me. Now, you follow him from the ground and I'll follow him from the trees. Don't attack unless it's absolutely necessary. Stick to the plan."

"We'll see," Fu replied. He leaped silently out of the tree and took cover in a thick bush.

Malao tightened his fist around the spores and jumped into a nearby tree. He paused a few moments before springing into a third. Malao looked down.

Commander Woo was directly below him, opening the leather bag.

Malao watched as Commander Woo set the forked stick aside and eased himself onto the ground. He rummaged through the leather bag and removed the pouch of dragon bone, a small spoon, and the goblet. The Commander steadied the goblet on the ground and opened the silk pouch clumsily. He dumped a spoonful of the powder into the goblet and retied the pouch. As Commander Woo put the pouch and the spoon back into the leather bag, Malao dropped out of the tree and wiggled from head to toe in the half-light, his grassy outline shimmering.

"What do you think you are going to do with that powder?" Malao asked in the same ghastly voice he had used back at Cangzhen.

Commander Woo looked up and his entire body jolted. His mouth moved like he was talking, but no words came out.

Malao choked back a giggle. "I see you've heard of me, Commander. Your men knew I would return if they mentioned me to anyone."

"W-what does that have to do with me?" Commander Woo asked. "I didn't tell anyone about you."

"Liar!" Malao said. "I know you told that witchcraft amateur Ying about me. Say goodbye to this life, Commander Woo. I have come to swallow your soul!"

"No!" Commander Woo said. "P-please, I'll do anything you ask."

"Anything?"

"Yes!"

"Give me the dragon bone."

Commander Woo paused. "B-but it doesn't belong to me. It's Major Ying's."

"Would you like me to summon the spirit of the dragon that once called those bones his own?" Malao asked. "I'm sure he'd be happy to meet the man who is making a drink with his remains."

"No!" Commander Woo said. "What if—"

A low growl erupted from a large bush behind Commander Woo. The Commander spun around.

Malao quickly brushed the mushroom spores from his hand into the goblet.

Commander Woo looked back at Malao. "W-what was that noise?"

"The dragon, you fool," Malao said, trying desperately not to giggle. Fu was supposed to have hissed, not growled.

Commander Woo's eyes widened.

A voice suddenly rang out from the direction of the camp. "Commander Woo? Is that you?"

Malao recognized that voice. It was Tonglong.

Commander Woo turned toward the voice, and Malao disappeared into the undergrowth.

CHAPTER 19

"What's going on here?" Tonglong asked.

Commander Woo stood awkwardly, favoring his injured leg. He held the goblet in one hand and the forked stick in the other.

"You're up and walking around already, sir?" Commander Woo said. "Shouldn't you be recuperating from that blow you took to the head? I heard that the young monk called Fu used his Iron Head kung fu to—"

"I'm fine, Commander," Tonglong said. "Thank you for your concern. Now answer my question, please."

"I was about to prepare a special drink for Major Ying," Commander Woo said. "But I was, aahhh, sidetracked. I still need to catch a snake, so I'd better get going."

Tonglong looked in the goblet. "Snake blood and dragon bone?"

"Yes, sir," Commander Woo replied.

"*Foolish witchcraft mumbo jumbo*," Tonglong muttered.

"I beg your pardon, sir?"

"Never mind. Who were you talking to?"

"No one, sir," Commander Woo said. "I was, aahhh, talking to myself. I feel foolish that you heard me."

Tonglong looked Commander Woo in the eye. "Commander, have I ever lied to you?"

"No, sir. W-why do you ask?"

"Because I hold truth above all things," Tonglong said. "And I would be greatly disappointed if I ever learned that one of my peers lied to me."

"Your peers, sir?" Commander Woo said.

Tonglong smiled and put his hand on Commander Woo's shoulder. "Look, Commander. I know that I'm technically Major Ying's number one man and you're technically his number two. But the way I see it, we're equals. We have the same responsibilities and we do the same things. We're peers in my eyes. I would never lie to a peer for any reason. Peers need to stick together."

Commander Woo looked at the ground and shuffled his feet. "You're absolutely right. Now I feel even more foolish. I have a confession to make—I was talking to a spirit."

Tonglong's eyebrows raised. "You were? Well, that's

interesting. It didn't happen to be the same spirit the men saw on the roof at Cangzhen, did it?"

Commander Woo snapped his head up. "Yes! How did you know?"

"I'm assuming it came after you because you talked to Major Ying about it. Spirits don't like that."

"I know!" Commander Woo said. "It's a good thing you came along when you did. You scared it off. It was very unhappy."

"I'm glad I could be of service," Tonglong said. "Now, you'd better get going. Major is expecting his drink. He sent me to check up on you, you know." Tonglong patted Commander Woo on the back. "But don't worry, my friend. Your secret is safe with me. I won't tell a soul what just happened."

"Thank you, sir," Commander Woo said. "Thank you very much."

"Don't mention it," Tonglong replied. "Good luck finding a snake."

Commander Woo nodded and hobbled into the forest.

Tonglong watched him go, then tucked his long braid into his sash and squatted down. He lowered his face a hair's width above a small footprint in the dirt and inhaled. His nose recoiled, but the corners of his mouth turned up.

"Where's my drink?" Ying shouted.

"Coming!" Commander Woo replied. He limped

through the darkness toward Ying, who was sitting next to Tonglong in front of a roaring campfire.

Commander Woo stopped in front of Ying and cleared his throat. "If you don't mind my saying, sir, you still have a little time. It's not yet been one hour since the sun set. I'm sure of it."

"I believe you are correct," Ying said. "But unlike some people around here, I'd rather not wait until the last moment for everything."

"I am sorry, sir," Commander Woo said as he handed the goblet to Ying. "It is my first time preparing the drink. It took me longer than I thought. It will not happen again. I promise."

Ying smirked. "You weren't delayed by spirits, were you?"

Commander Woo stiffened. He glanced at Tonglong. Tonglong shook his head very slowly.

Ying laughed. "That was a joke, Commander. Relax! It seems reading the scrolls has put me in a fine mood. You have nothing to be concerned about. For once, you did your job. Not like our big failure Tonglong here."

Tonglong lowered his head.

Ying raised the goblet and flicked his forked tongue across his lips. "Here's to me." He drank the elixir in one gulp and ran his tongue around the inside of his mouth. "What kind of snake did you use?"

Commander Woo paused. "I'm not sure, sir. It was a brown ground dweller and had a triangular head

like all vipers. I am certain it was a poisonous variety.
Why do you ask?"

"The drink tastes a little different today. It must be
the snake. I usually use green tree snakes. I don't know
why, but I've always found them easy to get my hands
on." Ying held up a perfectly formed eagle-claw fist
and flexed his fingers. He laughed at his own joke.

Commander Woo laughed, too.

Tonglong smirked and rubbed the lump on his
head. "You certainly are a clever one, Major Ying." He
turned away from the campfire and stared off into the
trees.

CHAPTER 20

"How long do you think it's been?" Malao whispered.

"I don't know," Fu replied. "Several hours, I guess. They should all be asleep by now."

"I think so, too. Let's go."

Malao leaped down from their hiding place high in a large elm and landed silently on the dark forest floor. Fu landed next to him.

"You take the lead, Cat Eyes," Malao whispered. "I can hardly see a thing tonight. There are too many clouds covering the moon."

Fu grunted and began to stalk silently through the heavy brush. Malao followed close behind. As soon as Malao saw campfire flames in the distance, he took to the trees. The plan was for him to approach from above while Fu approached from below. Once one of them found the scrolls, that person would grab the scrolls and run. Hopefully, the other would be able to follow.

Malao located a suitable limb near the edge of Ying's camp and scooted out as far as his weight would allow. He lay down on his stomach and hugged the branch tight, glad that he had abandoned his itchy "spirit" costume in order to move more freely through the trees.

Almost immediately, Malao heard soft footfalls. He glanced down and saw a single soldier with a spear patrolling the camp perimeter. The soldier was walking slowly in Malao's direction.

Malao looked over at the campfire and was surprised to see Ying lying near it, fast asleep on the ground. No one else was around. Ying's men apparently had built the large campfire away from the main sleeping area. Malao had heard that travelers often did this in case animals were attracted to the lingering smells of cooking over the campfire.

Ying must have fallen asleep there and his men were afraid to move him, Malao thought. *He seems to be out cold. This is going to be easy.*

Malao let go of the tree branch with one arm and slowly removed the decorated stick from the folds of his robe. As he raised it up, rustling leaves caught his attention. He turned to see Fu burst out of the underbrush.

Malao looked back down at the soldier. The soldier assumed a defensive posture with his spear held out before him. Malao decided to give Fu a little assistance. He cleared his throat, making the soldier glance up.

At that same instant, Fu slammed his left shoulder into the soldier's chest. Malao watched Fu clamp his right hand over the soldier's mouth and kick the soldier's legs out from under him. It wasn't the most graceful technique Malao had ever seen, but it was effective. The soldier went down in a heap and Fu landed on top of him. Fu grabbed the man's spear with his free hand, wrenched it from the soldier's grasp, and tossed it aside.

As soon as Malao saw Fu clamp a tiger-claw fist around the soldier's throat, he leaped down from the tree and headed for Ying. Malao gripped his stick tight. He knew that Ying hated to be woken and would lash out violently at anyone who dared disturb him.

When he was two paces from Ying, Malao stopped. Ying's chest rose and fell steadily and his eyeballs raced around beneath closed eyelids. Malao wondered if Ying was dreaming about all the horrible things he had done at Cangzhen.

Malao shivered. He forced himself to take several deep breaths, then took another step toward Ying and lowered himself into a solid Horse Stance. Prepared to run—or fight, if necessary—Malao lifted one leg and stuck his bare foot beneath Ying's nose. He wiggled his toes. Ying didn't flinch.

Malao grinned. He leaned forward and reached into Ying's robe. Inside, he found the scrolls. Malao removed them and placed them in the folds of his own robe.

Someone cleared his throat and Malao flinched, nearly stumbling into Ying. It was Fu. He stood at the opposite end of the clearing, pointing off into the forest.

Malao nodded. He was about to join Fu when something shiny on the other side of the clearing caught his eye. Malao strained his vision and took several steps in that direction. He saw a soldier asleep in the shadows. The shiny object was the hilt of the man's straight sword reflecting the firelight.

Malao took a few more steps and the soldier groaned, rolling over. Malao held his breath.

A moment later, the soldier began to snore. Malao released a huge sigh of relief. He turned away from the sleeping soldier and ran off to join Fu, never noticing the man's extraordinarily long ponytail.

CHAPTER 21

"That was way too easy," Fu said, panting heavily. He stopped ahead of Malao on the dark forest trail.

Malao nearly crashed into Fu. "Careful, Pussycat. What are you doing?"

"Something strange is going on," Fu said. "I want to stop and think for a moment."

"Don't hurt yourself," Malao replied. He giggled.

Fu ignored the comment. He bent over and examined the ground. Malao leaned over next to him.

"Are you sure this is the right trail?" Malao asked.

"No," Fu said. "The cage was covered with blankets the whole time the soldiers carried me. However, the boot prints on this trail are fairly fresh. I think this is the trail that will lead us back to the village."

"Do you really think the Governor knows the way to Shaolin Temple?" Malao asked.

"I hope so. Otherwise, I don't know how we'll ever find it."

"Do you think—"

Fu stood and stared at Malao in the darkness. "Please stop with the questions, Malao. I'm trying to figure out what's going on with Ying."

"Ying?" Malao said. "Ying was out cold. Believe me."

"I believe he was out cold. Otherwise, he would have ripped your leg to shreds for sticking your nasty foot in his face. Still, something just doesn't feel right."

"What do you mean?" Malao asked.

"Think about it," Fu said. "The only thing between us and the scrolls was one lousy soldier. And why did they leave Ying by the fire like that?"

"Ying probably fell asleep there after drinking the mushroom spores and everyone was afraid to touch him. You know how much he hates to be woken."

"But why was there only one soldier on patrol?"

"I think there were supposed to be two," Malao said. "I saw another one sleeping in the shadows."

"What?" Fu said. "What did he look like?"

"I don't know," Malao replied. "It was dark."

"Did you notice *anything* about him? Was he short and stocky? Tall and skinny? Did he wear armor? Or an elegant robe?"

Malao shrugged his shoulders. "I don't know. All I saw was a straight sword. What does it matter?"

Fu slammed his fist into his palm. "Tonglong! I knew something was going on!"

"Tonglong?" Malao said. "Ying's number one man? Oh, yeah! He carries a straight sword."

"That's right," Fu said. "I bet Tonglong knew Ying was unconscious and that we would return. He was probably awake the whole time, making sure we got the scrolls."

"Making sure *we* got the scrolls?" Malao said. "You think Tonglong is on our side?"

"Maybe. Remember when he helped us escape in the forest by loosening my bindings and letting me head-butt him? Well, he really didn't have to. I never told you this, but Tonglong had already repaid his debt to me for sparing his life back at Cangzhen. After Ying killed Grandmaster, Ying was about to attack me again. However, Tonglong distracted him and I escaped. He saved my life and repaid the debt."

Malao scratched his head. "Maybe Tonglong didn't realize what he'd done at Cangzhen."

"I doubt it," Fu replied.

"Hey! Maybe Tonglong was a secret friend of Grandmaster's!"

"Don't start with that secret-operation nonsense, Malao. I heard enough of it from Hok."

"No, it may be true," Malao said. "I didn't get a chance to tell you, but I recognized the leader of the bandit gang Seh is now traveling with. I'm positive I saw him at Cangzhen four or five times with Grandmaster. You would remember him, too. He's a giant of a man." Malao paused. "I never saw Tonglong at Cangzhen, but he does remind me of someone. I just wish I could remember who. . . ."

Fu cocked his head to one side. "Now that you mention it, Tonglong reminds me of someone, too. Do you think Tonglong is some kind of spy working against Ying?"

"I don't know," Malao said. "You're the one who thinks more is going on. If you ask me, I think I had a great plan to steal the scrolls and it worked. You're just jealous." He giggled.

Fu shook his head and looked around. He yawned. "I'm getting tired, Malao. You want to take a break?"

Malao stretched. "I guess. Do you think it's safe?"

"I think so. If Tonglong wanted to get us, he would have come after us already. Ying didn't even flinch beneath your disgusting toes and the man I knocked out will probably stay unconscious until morning. As long as we don't sleep too long, we should be fine."

"All right, then," Malao said. "I *am* pretty tired."

"Me too," Fu replied. "I'm going to sleep on the ground. I don't think I can handle sleeping in a tree."

"Suit yourself," Malao said. "I'm going to find me a nice big oak."

"Hang on," Fu said. "Before you go, let me take a look at the scrolls."

Malao sprang backward on the trail. "I don't think so, Pussycat. It was my plan that got them back, so I'm

Monkey

猴

125

going to be the one to deliver them to the monks at Shaolin. You're not going to take all the credit." He grinned.

"I'm not going to steal them, Malao. I just want to make sure someone isn't toying with us."

"I'm not sure I believe you," Malao said, tapping his chin. "I tell you what. I'll look the scrolls over myself tonight, and maybe—if you're really, really nice to me—I'll let you take a peek when we get to the village. How's that sound?"

"Stop playing around. Just give me one, okay?"

"You're no fun," Malao said. He pulled a scroll from his robe and handed it to Fu.

Fu opened the scroll. "It looks like the real thing to me. I had to dry them out the other day, and I recognize this one." Fu rolled the scroll back up and reached out to return it to Malao.

Malao shook his head. "We should probably split them up in case something happens to one of us. You carry that one, and I'll carry the other two. All right?"

Fu's eyes widened. "What?"

"I know it's not nice to think about something bad happening to one of us, but—"

Every muscle in Fu's body tensed.

"Hey, are you okay?" Malao asked.

Fu took a deep breath. "Malao, how many scrolls did you take from Ying?"

"Three," Malao said, slowly backing away. "Why?"

Fu's eye filled with fury. "There are FOUR dragon scrolls, Banana Brain!"

CHAPTER 22

Ying woke to blurred vision and a fierce headache. He sat up and rubbed his eyes. As the world came into focus, he realized he wasn't in his tent. He was outside for some reason, next to the campfire. It was daylight, and a huge pot of *seefan*—rice porridge—was cooking over the fire. *Seefan* was the soldiers' morning meal.

Confused, Ying called out, "Number One Tonglong! Commander Woo! Captain Yue! Report to the campfire! Immediately!"

Ying stood on shaky legs. He felt dizzy and nauseated. It took every bit of strength he had to stop himself from throwing up.

Captain Yue arrived first. "Sir?" he said hesitantly.

"What is going on?" Ying asked.

Captain Yue fidgeted with his luxurious silk robe. "You fell asleep, sir."

"I fell asleep here?" Ying said. "Next to the fire?"

"Yes, sir. Last night. Don't you remember?"

"No."

Captain Yue turned away and stared off into the distance. "I wasn't here much, Major Ying. I spent most of yesterday evening getting a splint on my leg. If you'll recall, my leg was injured back at the village when my horse fell on it. Commander Woo had *his* leg treated first, so *I* had to wait. Perhaps if I had been treated first—"

"Stop your whining, Captain," Ying said. "Where is Commander Woo?"

"Coming, sir!" Commander Woo said as he appeared from the opposite direction. Tonglong was at his side. Soldiers began to slowly file in around them.

"We were looking for clues to what happened last night," Commander Woo said. "We believe the young monks are responsible."

"Responsible for what?" Ying asked.

Tonglong cleared his throat. "Check your robe, sir."

Ying looked down and saw that his robe was pulled open over his chest. His eyes narrowed. "The scrolls!"

"Yes, sir," Tonglong said. "As Commander Woo said, we believe the young monks are responsible. If you look where you were lying, you'll find tracks that are too small to have been made by an adult. We recently discovered matching tracks on the trail that leads back to the village. We believe the young monks took the scrolls from you and have since headed back to the village."

Ying scowled. "How could this have happened? Where was I while all this was going on?"

"You were asleep, sir," Tonglong said.

"And no one bothered to wake me?"

"We tried, sir," Commander Woo replied. "But you would not respond to any noise or physical contact. We believe you were drugged."

"Drugged?" Ying said. "Who would dare do such a thing?"

"Again, we put the blame on the young monks," Commander Woo said. "I may have to take part of the blame, too. Since you ate no dinner last night, we can only assume the dragon bone elixir I prepared for you was tainted."

Ying took a step toward Commander Woo. He popped his knuckles one at a time. "And how could that have happened, Commander?"

Commander Woo swallowed hard. "I—I left the goblet unattended for a few moments. Perhaps one of the monks slipped something into it while I was catching the snake."

Ying took another step toward Commander Woo.

"Wait, sir," Tonglong said hurriedly. "Not all was lost." He reached into his wide red sash and pulled out a scroll. He handed it to Ying.

"What's this?" Ying asked.

"It's a dragon scroll," Tonglong replied. "I found it

in your tent. You must have left it there before going to the campfire last night."

"Oh, really?" Ying said. "What were you doing in my tent without my permission?"

"Forgive me, sir," Tonglong said. "I was only looking for clues."

"Looking for clues?" Ying snapped. "Fu must have knocked something loose when he struck your head! How dare you enter my quarters uninvited? Give me one good reason why I shouldn't tear you apart right now?"

Tonglong leaned forward and whispered, "Because the men might view such action as excessive. There's a great risk of losing their respect."

"*Respect?*" Ying raised an eagle-claw fist, then paused. He remembered what he had read in the first dragon scroll. He scowled. In a low voice he said, "What do you suggest we do, then, Tonglong?"

"We must shift our focus to the young monks," Tonglong whispered. "Give the men a plan, and keep them thinking about only one thing—catching the boys."

Ying relaxed his fist. "What plan?"

"I suggest you lead the men to the village and capture the boys. I'll go to Shaolin Temple, just in case."

"*Shaolin?*" Ying said.

"Yes," Tonglong replied. "Though I am almost certain the young monks will head back to the village, they may go to Shaolin instead. I want to prevent that from happening. If I take my horse, I should be able to arrive well before them. I'll patrol the surrounding area and cut them off before they make it to the temple."

Ying ran his hand through his short black hair. "How will we communicate with you?"

Tonglong raised his voice slightly. "If you and the men stay at the village, I'll report to you there. In my opinion, the men could use a break. It might make sense to let them rest for a few weeks. Some fresh food and sleep would do them good."

Ying glanced at two nearby soldiers. The men looked exhausted.

Ying turned to Tonglong. "Leave. I'll see you at the village."

Tonglong turned and walked away. Ying frowned and looked at Captain Yue. "You were at the village. Why do you think the boys would return there? Aren't these the same villagers who captured Fu and took the scrolls from him?"

"Yes," Captain Yue said. "But I believe the villagers have had a change of heart. There's also the Drunkard to consider—"

"Who?"

"There was a drunkard," Captain Yue said. "He is a big, powerful man and an excellent fighter. He stood up for the boy called Fu. In fact, he's the one who injured my horse and caused it to fall on top of my leg. We shot him with a *qiang*, but he may have survived. If the boys are looking for allies, this man would be a strong one. Perhaps they went back to find him."

Ying looked at Commander Woo. Commander Woo shrugged his shoulders. Ying spat.

Ying turned back to Captain Yue. "Tell me more about this Drunkard. What did he look like?"

Captain Yue began to fidget. "He had long, tangled hair and a scraggly beard. Also, his clothes were in tatters and he spoke with a deep, gravelly voice."

Ying's eyebrows raised. "What did he fight like?"

"Excuse me, sir?"

"Did his fighting techniques resemble the movements of a specific animal? Like a python, or perhaps a bear?"

"If I had to guess, I would say a tiger, sir," Captain Yue replied. "Albeit a drunken one."

Ying grinned and the grooves in his face deepened. "A *tiger*? You don't say. . . ."

"**W**ake up," Fu said in a gruff voice. "We need to get moving."

Malao opened his eyes and squinted in the morning sun. He looked around and scratched his head. He was high in the slender, sticky arms of a pine tree. This was not a tree he would normally climb, let alone sleep in.

Malao looked down at Fu and remembered what had happened the previous night. Fu had chased him up there!

"Come on, Malao," Fu said. "I'm not going to hurt you. I promise."

Malao hesitated. "You're not upset about the scrolls anymore? I thought you were going to kill me last night."

"Yes, I'm upset about the scrolls," Fu replied. "But it wasn't your fault. You didn't know how many scrolls there were. I probably should have told you there were four."

"Whoa," Malao said, wide-eyed. "Was that an apology?"

"Don't push me, Malao."

Malao giggled and climbed down, carefully avoiding the tree's irritating needles. By the time he hit the ground, Fu was quite a ways up the trail. Malao jogged to Fu's side.

"I swear Ying only had three scrolls in his robe," Malao said. "He was probably reading the fourth one somewhere else. He must have put it away. Or maybe he set it down and someone else picked it up. Or maybe—"

"Or maybe you could stop talking about it," Fu interrupted.

"Oh, sorry," Malao said. "How about if we talk about something else? Tell me what you've been doing. Did you miss me?" He grinned.

"Can we just walk in silence for once?"

"Come on, Fu. You've had several different adventures, and you haven't told me about any of them. Tell me how you defeated Tonglong."

Fu didn't respond.

"All right," Malao said. "Then tell me about the young tiger. Or tell me how you met the Governor. Or—"

"That's enough, Malao. I told you, I don't want to talk. Please."

"But—"

"No."

Malao pouted. "Fine, then how about if I tell you about my adventures with a huge bandit named Bear."

"No," Fu said. "I just want a little peace and quiet."

Malao stopped and put his hands on his hips. "I'm not going to stop until you tell me at least one story. Why don't you tell me about some of the people I might meet in the village? Did you meet anyone our age?"

Fu stopped and turned back to face Malao. "The Governor has a son our age. Everyone calls him Ho, but I wouldn't be surprised if his name was actually Ho Dao. Are you satisfied?"

"*Ho Dao?*" Malao said. "'Forgiving'? What does he have to forgive you for?"

"I don't want to talk about it."

"Come on, Fu. Tell me how you met the Governor's son."

"No. It's a very long story."

"Just give me the short version," Malao said. "You could—"

Fu growled and leaned his face in close to Malao's. "I smashed a spear shaft into Ho's ear so hard, I nearly made him deaf for life. And you know what he did to deserve it? Nothing. How do you like that story?"

Malao began to squirm. "Sorry, Fu. I . . . I didn't know."

Fu stared hard at Malao. "That's right. You *don't* know. When I say I don't want to talk, I really mean it.

Especially when it comes to Ho. I did something wrong and it makes me feel terrible."

"I'm sorry," Malao said again.

Fu grunted and walked away.

Malao waited a bit before following Fu up the trail. He wanted to give Fu plenty of space.

Malao followed Fu this way the rest of the morning. On several occasions, Malao thought he caught a glimpse of something watching him from high in the trees. Something white. Over time, however, Malao realized that he was just imagining things. The patches he hoped were monkey fur turned out to be sunlight.

Malao really missed the white monkey. Part of him wanted to believe that his new friend would be waiting for him at the village, since that's where they'd been headed when they'd last seen each other. But another part of him wondered why the white monkey would even bother. After all, it had been shot trying to help him. Malao wouldn't blame the white monkey one bit if it wanted nothing more to do with him.

Malao sighed. Lost in his thoughts, he didn't notice that Fu had stopped on the trail.

"Ooof!" Malao muttered as he slammed into Fu. Fu didn't seem to notice. His head was cocked to one side and he appeared to be listening to something farther up the trail. Malao listened, too. After a moment, Malao thought he heard voices. Aggressive voices.

"Come on!" Fu said excitedly. "We're almost there!"

"Are you sure this is the right place?" Malao asked. "Those people don't sound very nice—"

"You'll see," Fu said, grabbing Malao by the collar of his robe. "Follow me!"

As Malao followed, he paid close attention to the sounds ahead. To his surprise, the closer he got, the more it sounded like group kung fu drills back at Cangzhen.

Malao and Fu soon reached a wall of tall bushes that ran parallel to the trail. Fu motioned for Malao to stay close and pointed to a section of the bushes that had been trampled. It looked as if a horse had barreled through there. Fu walked through the trampled area into a huge square that was almost completely surrounded by the same tall bushes.

Malao followed Fu and saw nearly one hundred children practicing kung fu. The practice session was led by a large boy with intense eyes and wild black hair. He was tall and powerful, and his heavy gray peasant's robe *snapped* loudly with every punch he threw. Malao noticed immediately that the boy's hands were not folded into typical fists. Instead, they were crudely formed tiger claws.

Fu approached the large boy from behind. "Where did you learn to punch like that?" Fu asked. "You punch like a girl."

Without turning around, the boy replied, "If you mean that my punches resemble those of the girl who lives next door to me, I'll take that as a compliment."

Fu smiled. "She taught you well."

The large boy stopped his punching and turned to face Fu. He grinned and slapped Fu on the shoulder. "You're amazing, Fu! How on earth did you escape?"

Fu nodded in Malao's direction. "My little brother helped me."

The large boy raised his eyebrows.

Malao shrugged.

"My name is Ma," the boy said to Malao. "Nice to meet you."

"Nice to meet you, too," Malao replied. "My name is Malao, but Fu likes to call me by other names. What was that last one you used, Fu? *Banana Brain?*"

Fu shook his head. "I don't remember. But if you keep this up, the next one will be *Broken Monkey.*"

Malao giggled and glanced at Ma. Ma wasn't laughing.

"*Monkey?*" Ma asked.

"Ah, yeah," Malao replied. "My name means 'monkey' in Cantonese. Why?"

Ma stared at Malao but didn't say a word.

Eager to change the subject, Malao said, "Hey, did Fu show you how to punch like that?"

"Sort of," Ma replied. He looked at Fu and seemed to relax a little. "Fu showed each of us a different kung fu technique, and now we're teaching our moves to each other. It's really great."

Malao laughed. "Yeah, I guess it would be if everyone was a giant like you and this overgrown pussycat. Tiger-style techniques are perfect for overpowering people. Unfortunately, most kids are like me—small."

Ma's eyes narrowed. "The technique Fu taught me helped save a life."

"Oh . . . I'm sorry," Malao said, raising his hands. "I

was only joking. Well, half joking. If you'd like, I could teach you a few monkey-style techniques and show you what I mean."

"*Monkey-style?*" Ma said. "I don't think so."

A small boy from the group suddenly called out, "I want to learn! Teach me!"

Malao grinned at the boy and released a dramatic sigh. "I'd love to teach you some moves, my friend, but I'm afraid I might not have enough energy. I'm famished." Malao dropped to the ground, pretending to faint.

The small boy laughed.

"Just ignore him," Fu said, shaking his head. "He'll get up eventually."

The small boy laughed again. "I think he's funny!"

Ma looked at Fu. "What about you? Are you hungry?"

"You could say that," Fu replied. "I haven't eaten anything since your mother's Greasy Goose."

"What?" Ma said. "That was a day and a half ago! Hang on, I'll be right back. Four chicken buns coming right up."

Malao snapped his head in Fu's direction and made a sour face. Fu called out to Ma, "Make that two chicken buns and two plain buns, please. Malao doesn't eat meat."

"It figures," Ma mumbled as he headed for the bun vendor's shop. "Monkeys are nothing but trouble...."

A few moments later, Ma returned. "These are compliments of the bun vendor. He's very busy now, but he said he will come see you later, Fu. He said he wants to 'commend you for your bravery' yesterday morning. He's impressed that you put your life on the line for the village."

Malao glanced questioningly at Fu.

Fu shrugged. "Maybe I'll tell you about it some-time," he said. "Right now, let's eat." Fu turned to Ma. "Thanks for the food."

"Don't mention it," Ma replied.

"Yeah, thanks a lot!" Malao said. He dug in and fin-ished off his buns in no time. He burped loudly. "Aahhh! Now, who's ready to learn some *real* kung fu?"

"Me!" shouted the small boy, along with several other boys and girls in the village square.

Malao looked over at Fu and saw that he was deep in conversation with Ma. It looked like they would be there for a while.

"Okay," Malao said to the group of children as he stood. "I'm assuming you have all stretched out your muscles, right?"

"Yes," the group replied.

"Great," Malao said. "Did Fu teach you the Horse Stance? You know, the basic beginning position where you sort of squat down with your legs about shoulder-width apart?"

"Yes."

Malao grinned. "That's good. Keep practicing it because it's an important exercise. However, we won't be using it today."

"So you're not going to teach us how to fight?" the small boy asked.

"Not exactly," Malao replied. "I said I was going to teach you some monkey-style kung fu. Kung fu isn't always about fighting. In fact, most monkey-style followers don't even like to fight. They usually prefer to run away. Many times the winner of a fight still gets hurt, and I know I'd rather run away healthy than win a fight and end up with a broken arm or leg. The number one rule is to walk away from a fight, or run away if you have to. Understand?"

"I guess so," the small boy said. "But what are you supposed to do if you can't run away? What if you have no choice?"

"If you're small like me, you have to be prepared to play dirty," Malao said with a devilish grin. "If you ever find yourself in a corner and you're feeling afraid, show it. It will help make your opponent feel overconfident. And if you have no choice but to fight back, you should strike and retreat. No one can hurt you if you're not there. After a swift kick-and-punch combination, run away and don't look back. It is said that monkeys fight with four hands. That means use your feet and your fists simultaneously. Does that make sense?"

The small boy scratched his head. "Yes, but what kind of punch should we use? And what kind of kick?"

"You could use whatever Fu showed you, or you could make up your own. A lot of monkey-style moves are made up as you go along, especially if you're attacking the eyes or throat. Just do whatever comes to mind first, then get out of there as fast as you can."

"Could you show us some moves?" the small boy asked. "Please?"

Malao smiled and looked at Fu. Fu was still talking to Ma.

"Hey, Fu," Malao interrupted. "How long do you think we'll be here?"

"I don't know," Fu replied. "I don't want to stay too long. It's only a matter of time before Ying—"

Fu suddenly stopped talking. He was staring at the bun vendor's shop across the square. In front of the shop was a large man with long, tangled hair and a scraggly beard. One of his lower legs was bandaged, and he leaned on a crutch.

"I'll be right back," Fu said hurriedly. "You stay here and conduct some more monkey business, Malao." Fu nodded to Ma and raced off toward the man.

Malao shrugged and looked at the group. "Anybody want to learn how to make a Hammer Fist?"

CHAPTER 24

Malao was having a hard time concentrating. Though his students were eager to learn and he was excited to be sharing his knowledge with them, he just couldn't seem to keep his eyes off Fu and the large, scraggly man in front of the bun vendor's shop. It was uncanny how Fu's body style mirrored the big man's, and how often Fu and the man used the same gestures as they spoke. Curiosity soon got the best of Malao.

"Everybody keep practicing your Hammer Fists," Malao said to the village children. "I'll be right back." He scurried over to join Fu.

The large man stopped talking in mid-sentence as

Malao approached. He grinned and said, "Hello, little one. You must be Malao."

"Aahhh, yeah," Malao said. "And you are—"

"A friend," Fu answered. "He's just a friend."

The big man smiled and put his hand on Fu's shoulder. "I have been called many things in my time," the man said to Malao. "But most recently people have been calling me the Drunkard."

"Oh," Malao said. "I'm sorry."

The Drunkard laughed. "That's okay. I don't mind." He looked at Fu. "I'm not really a drunkard, you know. I've been passing myself off as one the past several years because I've found that people tend to leave me alone this way. Since that's what I want, I keep the act going."

"But why would you want to be left alone?" Malao asked.

"That, my little friend, is a very long story," the Drunkard said. He looked at Fu again. "I have so many stories to share."

Fu's eyebrows raised. "Do any of them have anything to do with being a warrior monk?"

"As a matter of fact, yes," the Drunkard replied.

"I knew it!" Fu said. "I knew you were a warrior monk when I saw you fight. How come you aren't living in a temple?"

"I left."

"Why?" Malao asked.

"That is a very, very long story," the Drunkard replied.

"That's okay," Malao said. "I love stories! Especially stories about warrior monks."

"All right," the Drunkard said. "I left the temple because I fell in love with a woman. As you probably know, that's not allowed. We wanted to marry and start a family, so I had to leave."

"Really?" Malao asked. "Are you still married?"

The Drunkard lowered his head. "No. She died giving birth to our first child. It's been quite . . . difficult for me."

"Is that why you want to be alone?" Malao asked.

"Yes," the Drunkard said. "Partially."

"That's really sad," Malao said. "How long ago was that?"

The Drunkard looked at Fu. "Twelve years."

Malao's eyes widened. *Fu was twelve years old!* He glanced at Fu.

Fu looked down.

"Why don't I get right to the point," the Drunkard said. "I've been thinking a lot about you, Fu. You remind me so much of myself. Over the years, I've come to the conclusion that I am the way I am partly because I grew up in a temple without ever knowing my parents—just like you. It had an impact on me. It still does, I suppose. If you don't mind my asking, do you ever think about your parents?"

Fu shrugged. "Not really. I always assumed they were dead."

The Drunkard's eyebrows raised. "Why did you assume that?"

"Because I was taken to Cangzhen as a baby," Fu said. "If my parents weren't dead, it would mean that I had been abandoned. What kind of parent would—"

Fu stopped suddenly and looked up. He blushed. The Drunkard blushed, too.

"I'm sorry—" Fu began to say.

The Drunkard cleared his throat. "No, I'm the one who's sorry, Fu." He began to limp away.

Malao punched Fu in the arm. "Say something!"

Fu shrugged.

"Argh!" Malao said. "Stubborn Pussycat!"

The Drunkard hobbled around the corner of the bun vendor's shop without looking back.

"**W**hy didn't you say something?" Malao asked Fu.

"I don't know," Fu replied.

"What do you mean you don't know?"

"I just don't know," Fu said. He kicked the ground.

"Are you all right?" Malao asked.

"Yeah," Fu said. "I'm fine."

"How come you never told me about the Drunkard?"

Fu's voice lowered. "I don't want to talk about it, Malao."

"Sorry," Malao said. He patted Fu on the shoulder. "Do you want to get going?"

"Soon," Fu said.

"Okay," Malao said. "I'll be right back." He walked

over to the group of children in the center of the sunny village square. "All right, everyone, class is over," Malao announced. "Get yourselves some water, and don't forget what I taught you!"

The village children began talking excitedly among themselves and filed out of the square.

"Fu!" someone called out.

A skinny boy was walking into the square. He wore an elegant silk robe and looked very fragile, like a piece of fine porcelain. In his hand was a small silk pouch. Ma was at his side.

Fu seemed to come out of his trance. "Hello, Ho!" he said, and walked over to Malao.

Malao did a double take. He leaned toward Fu and whispered, "*That's* the kid you whacked with the spear?"

Fu swatted at Malao's head. Malao ducked.

"Hey, what was that for?" Malao asked.

Ma stepped up to Malao. "Did you just say something about my friend Ho?"

"Aahhh . . ."

Ma bent down toward Malao as though he was about to say more, but then he took a quick step back. His eyes narrowed. "Where did you get that stick?"

Malao glanced down and saw part of his decorated stick poking out of his robe. "This?" he replied. "It comes from Cangzhen."

Ma took another step back. "No, it doesn't."

"Sure it does," Malao said, pulling the stick out of his robe. "I've been practicing with it for years. You can hold it if you want."

"I don't want anything to do with that stick," Ma said. "Or you." He turned to Ho. "Come on, let's go."

Ho shook his head. "I want to talk to Fu. I'll come find you later. Okay?"

Ma snorted. He nodded to Ho and then Fu, then walked away.

Malao slipped his stick back in his robe and looked at Ho. "What's wrong with him?"

"He doesn't like monkeys," Ho replied. "And I think you . . . remind him of someone."

"Who's that?" Fu asked.

"The Monkey King," Ho said.

Malao twitched. "What? Why?"

"People say the Monkey King carries a stick like that," Ho said.

"You mean the monkey king of legend?" Fu asked. "He carried an iron staff that could magically change size, not a wooden stick."

"No," Ho said. "Not that monkey king. There is a famous thief in these parts whose nickname is the Monkey King because he's a monkey-style kung fu master. Also, he supposedly lives with a troop of monkeys."

Malao's heart began to race. "He's a thief? What does he steal?"

"Gold," Ho replied.

Malao twitched again.

"People say he's obsessed with it," Ho continued. "They say he'll stop at nothing to steal any shipment he comes across."

"Who ships gold around here?" Fu asked.

"Tax collectors," Ho said.

"But tax collectors take money from poor people, right?" Malao said. "Why is stealing from a tax collector a bad thing?"

Ho lowered his head. "Ma's father was a tax collector. He was killed delivering a shipment of gold."

Malao swallowed hard. An uncomfortable silence filled the square. He looked at Ho and noticed the silk pouch Ho carried. Desperate to change the subject, Malao said, "Excuse me, Ho? Do you mind if I ask what's in the bag?"

Ho looked up. "Oh, I almost forgot. It's blood-moss. When I heard you two had arrived, I ran to get some in case you needed it. I remembered Fu had some poking out of his cheek the last time he was here."

Ho held the pouch out to Malao.

"No thanks," Malao said. "I'm not injured. Besides, that stuff doesn't work for me or anyone I know except Fu. They say it's some kind of rare family trait."

"So I've heard," Ho replied. "It doesn't work for me, either. Here." Ho tossed the pouch to Fu. "I hope you never need it, but take it just in case."

"Thank you," Fu said as he tied the pouch to his sash. Fu looked over at Malao, who was fiddling with a small pouch on his own sash. "What's that?" Fu asked. "I didn't notice it before."

Malao looked down and smirked. "Oh, just a little something I borrowed from a bandit named Bear—"

"What's this about a bandit named Bear?" A man wearing an elegant robe just like Ho's walked around the wall of bushes. He had a strong chin and a kind face.

Fu smiled. "Hello, Governor."

Malao's eyes widened.

"Hello, Fu," the Governor said. "And hello to you, too, Malao."

Malao scratched his head. "Hello, sir."

"I just saw Ma," the Governor said. "He seems pretty upset."

Malao lowered his head. "I know. I'm really sorry to hear about his father."

"His father was a good man," the Governor said. "It's terrible that his life was taken by bandits."

Malao looked up. "Bandits? I thought the Monkey King killed him."

The Governor shook his head. "Nobody has ever proved that. No one I know has even *seen* the Monkey King. But it's a proven fact that bandits make a habit of intercepting gold shipments. Some bandits even go so far as to steal gold trinkets from people's homes as they sleep. The Monkey King is rumored to live in this region, but I've always dismissed him as a wives' tale people use to explain unexplainable thefts. That is, until today."

"W-why do you say that?" Malao asked, suddenly nervous.

"Well, because of you, quite frankly. You don't happen to know him, do you?"

"No!" Malao said. "W-what's going on?"

The Governor raised his hands. "There is no reason to get excited, little one. You are obviously too young to be him. I only ask because I thought he might be a relative of yours. You are a small, dark-skinned jokester—just like he supposedly is. Also, there is the stick Ma said you carry."

Fu looked at the Governor. "My brother is an orphan, just like me. He's no thief, and he has no relatives."

"I believe he may never have *met* any of his relatives," the Governor said. "But that does not mean he does not have any. I have one more piece of information to share. They say the Monkey King has trained a troop of monkeys to do his work since he's gotten older. The troop is rumored to be led by a large albino with a single eye." The Governor pointed to a tall tree just beyond the hedge around the square. "Look."

Malao gasped. In the tree was his friend the white monkey, staring straight at him. It shifted nervously from foot to foot and pointed down the trail he and Fu had followed to the village.

A voice called out in the distance, "Where is the Governor?"

Malao recognized that voice. It belonged to Ying!

CHAPTER 26

153

"That's Major Ying, isn't it?" the Governor asked.

Malao nodded. Fu growled.

"Ho, go warn the villagers that soldiers are returning," the Governor whispered. He looked at Malao and Fu. "You two, follow me."

They ran around to the back of the bun vendor's shop and ducked behind several large barrels. The Governor spoke in a low voice. "You will have to leave as soon as possible. I will do my best to stall Major Ying while you make your escape."

"Thank you, Governor," Malao said. Fu nodded.

"You are most welcome. Do you know where you will go?"

"We were going to ask if someone from your

village could show us the way to Shaolin Temple," Malao said.

"Shaolin?" the Governor replied. "That is a fine idea. The monks there can protect you."

"Yes," Fu said. "Plus we can give them the scrolls. Or most of the scrolls, anyway. We managed to steal three back from Ying."

"Good for you!" the Governor said. "I wish I could take you there myself, but I must remain here for now. Perhaps we can come up with a quick plan to have one of the villagers take you."

"How far is Shaolin from here?" Malao asked.

"It's only about ten days' travel by foot—"

"Ten days!" Malao said. "By the time we find it, Ying will catch up to us and—"

The barrel next to Malao shifted sideways. Malao looked up and found himself staring at Ying's carved face.

"When are you going to learn to keep your big mouth shut, Malao?" Ying said. "Get up!"

As Malao began to stand, he saw a large shadow pass over Ying from behind. Two beefy arms dropped over Ying's chest, pinning his arms to his sides. Malao heard the air slowly being squeezed out of Ying's lungs.

"RUN!" shouted a deep, gravelly voice from behind Ying's head. It was the Drunkard.

Malao turned to run, but Fu didn't budge.

The Drunkard's voice boomed again. "I said *run*, Fu!"

Fu stood frozen, his eyes locked on the Drunkard's.

Ying smirked. Hushed words drifted on the current of air pouring out of his mouth.

"Say goodbye to your new friend, Pussycat."

Ying lifted one bare foot and raked his long, curved toenails across the bandage covering the Drunkard's calf. The Drunkard faltered as the bandage tore away and the wound opened wide. Malao stared openmouthed at a large plug of bloodmoss that popped out of the hole in the Drunkard's leg.

Fu took a step forward.

"I'll handle this!" the Drunkard grunted. "Now— ARRRGH!"

Ying dug a long-nailed eagle-claw fist into each of the Drunkard's thighs. At the same time he opened his mouth wide and clamped his sharp teeth down on one of the Drunkard's forearms.

The Drunkard roared and released Ying, swinging one arm mightily across his body. A huge tiger-claw fist met the side of Ying's head. Ying dropped to his knees.

"I'll be fine," the Drunkard growled. "Now run, Fu! And don't look back!"

"But—"

"GO!"

Malao grabbed Fu's arm and pulled as hard as he could. To his surprise, Fu gave in. Together they raced around to the front of the bun vendor's shop. A line of soldiers stood between them and the trees.

"Angry Tiger Tosses Monkey!" Malao shouted.

Fu grunted and put his hands on his hips as he ran

full force toward the soldiers. Malao leaped onto Fu's back and used Fu's hands as footholds. He took a step up and placed one foot on each of Fu's shoulders. Fu grabbed one of Malao's ankles with each hand. When they were three paces from the line of soldiers, Fu shouted, "Now!"

Malao bent his knees and pushed off with all his might as Fu thrust his arms up and released Malao's ankles. Malao soared high over one of the soldiers and the careless man looked up. Fu slammed into the man, knocking him flat on his back. Fu stomped hard on the man's groin and barreled into the underbrush. Malao caught a tree limb with one hand and swung himself up into the treetops. Both boys instantly disappeared. The white monkey raced into the forest after them.

CHAPTER 27

"Fu, slow down," Malao said several hours later. "I think we're safe now."

Fu slowed to a fast walk and looked up at Malao and the white monkey high in the treetops. "Do you have any idea where we are?" he asked.

"No," Malao replied. "You want me to climb higher and take a look around?"

Fu stopped and bent over, panting heavily. "Yeah. See if you can find some water, too. I'm dying of thirst."

"Hang on," Malao said. He climbed higher and broke through the canopy with the white monkey at his side. The warm evening sun hit his face and he paused, filling his lungs with clean, fresh air. He turned to the monkey and patted its head. "It's nice up here, huh?" The monkey seemed to smile and nod. Malao smiled back.

The white monkey scratched the scab on the side of its head and Malao glanced at the larger scab on the monkey's arm. He remembered that his new friend had been injured while trying to protect him. He would never forget that.

The white monkey stopped scratching and stared at something in the distance. Malao followed its gaze. Not too far away, he saw a break in the trees. It snaked through the forest for many *li*. A river. Perfect.

Malao turned around in a complete circle and realized he had no idea where they were. He shrugged his shoulders and patted the monkey's head again. "Keep an eye out for danger. Let me know if you see anything suspicious." As Malao climbed down, the white monkey remained where it was, scanning the area.

Malao found Fu sitting on a large rock with his head in his hands.

"Let's go," Malao said. "I don't know where we are, but there's a river not too far away."

"Okay," Fu mumbled, but he didn't move.

"Are you all right?" Malao asked.

Fu pulled his hands slowly off his face and sighed. "Yeah, I'm fine."

"You don't look fine."

"I said *I'm fine,* Malao."

Malao scratched his head. "I wonder what happened to the Drunkard."

Fu looked up. "Can you do me a favor? Please don't call him the Drunkard anymore, okay?"

"Sure," Malao said. "What should I call him, then?"

"I don't know."

"How about if I just call him your father?"

Fu put his face back in his hands. "I don't think so."

"Why not?" Malao asked.

"Because there's no proof that he's my father, that's why not."

"Oh, come on, Fu. You can't be serious."

Fu looked up at Malao. "I'm dead serious."

"I would be proud if he was my father," Malao said, "no matter what people call him. He saved us."

"I know," Fu said. "I was there, remember?"

"Well, doesn't that mean something?"

"Of course it does. I just feel . . ." Fu shook his head. "I don't know how I feel."

"That's all right," Malao said, patting Fu's shoulder. "I've been thinking a lot about the Monkey King and how he might be . . . you know . . . *my* father. At least we know your father is a nice guy. If I knew my father was a nice guy, I would—"

"That's enough," Fu said, shrugging off Malao. "I know you're just trying to help, but I want to be alone right now."

"Fine," Malao said, standing up. "I guess I'll head over to that river alone and take a nice, long drink of cool, refreshing—"

"Goodbye, Malao."

"Suit yourself, Pussycat. You better hope I don't get

lost on my way back. It would be a shame if you didn't have me around to talk to anymore." Malao grinned.

"Yeah, that would be a real shame," Fu said. "Unfortunately, I'm sure your little friend would find you and guide you right back here."

Malao rolled his eyes.

Fu sighed. "I wish one of the villagers was here to guide us to Shaolin—"

Malao suddenly jumped high into the air and he clapped his hands. "A guide! Of course! Why didn't I think of that sooner?"

"What are you talking about?" Fu asked.

"Watch this," Malao said. He looked up into the treetops and waved his arms. The white monkey scurried down and over to Malao's side. Malao looked the monkey straight in the eye. "Can you take us to Shaolin Temple?"

The white monkey seemed to smile and grabbed Malao's hand. It squeezed three times, then scurried off. Malao giggled happily.

"How about that!" Malao said. "You wished for a guide, and now we have one! Come on, Fu!" Malao raced after the monkey.

"Hey!" Fu called out as he ran after them. "I wished for a *villager*!"

CHAPTER 28

One day later, Malao found himself wishing for a few things of his own. First and foremost was a large hat to shield him from the heavy rain. A dry robe would be nice, too. Preferably one without singed holes in the backside.

As they trudged toward Shaolin Temple, the rain came down in buckets, soaking Malao, Fu, and the white monkey to the bone. Malao did his best to look at the bright side. At least the downpour would wash away what few footprints they left, making it all but impossible for Ying and his men to track them.

The following day wasn't much better, nor the day after that. There were enough breaks in the storm to squeeze in a few meals of roasted mushrooms, but for the most part Malao found himself cold, wet, and hungry. He was itchy, too. Black, prickly hair had begun to sprout on his head.

To make matters worse, Fu was acting strange. He was extremely quiet and grumpy. Malao kept his distance.

By the fourth day, the sun finally began to shine again. Malao noticed that the change in the weather brought about a change in Fu. Fu began to talk again. Of course, most of it was complaints about the itchy black hair on his own large head, but Malao would take complaints over silence anytime.

Malao told Fu about his numerous adventures. He told him about the bandits, who, like the Governor had mentioned, had huge amounts of gold. He also explained how he had helped Hok retrieve Grandmaster's body. They talked for hours about what they thought Seh and Hok might be doing and debated over where their oldest brother, Long, might have disappeared to.

After nearly a week, Fu began to share some of his adventures. He described in great detail his tiger-hook-sword battle with Tonglong and how he originally came to possess the dragon scrolls. He also talked about how he had become blood brothers with the young tiger that had helped him, Malao, and Hok escape Tonglong in the forest. Fu even told Malao about the villagers and how the Drunkard had been shot trying to rescue him from Ying's number three man, Captain Yue.

Still, Fu never wanted to talk about the Drunkard in depth, and he always changed the subject whenever Malao brought up the Monkey King. It seemed any kind of father talk was off-limits as far as Fu was concerned. Malao didn't push.

Malao noticed that if there was one topic that really seemed to get Fu talking, it was Ying. Malao and Fu spent hour after hour arguing about where they thought Ying might appear next. In the end, they agreed that it really didn't matter where Ying showed up. They were headed to Shaolin Temple together, and nothing was going to stop them.

Nearly ten days after they had left the village, Malao decided Fu was finally back to his old self. It was a mixed blessing.

"I am so hungry!" Fu said. "Could you *please* ask our tour guide to find us something to eat?"

"Quit your complaining, Pussycat," Malao replied. "I'm sure they'll have plenty to eat at Shaolin."

"Yeah, if we ever make it there," Fu said. "Are you sure your friend knows where he's going? I don't see any sign of a temple. In fact, I haven't seen anything but trees and the back of your fuzzy head for days. We're not even on a trail. We're just following some one-eyed monkey through the forest. We should be there by now. The Governor said Shaolin was ten days away."

"The Governor probably traveled on a road," Malao said. "We've been walking through the forest."

"Yeah, but the Governor probably stopped and rested for a reasonable period of time every night. We've been traveling almost nonstop the whole time. Maybe we should look for a road."

"No," Malao said. "Someone might see us and report us to Ying. This is the best way to travel."

Fu shook his head. "I bet we're hopelessly lost. I bet—"

The white monkey suddenly stopped up ahead and stared back at Fu. It seemed to snicker.

Malao grinned. "Satisfied?"

"Satisfied with what?" Fu asked.

"Look." Malao pointed through the trees. Ahead was a clearing that appeared to contain numerous stone structures. Each one was tall and skinny and pointed to the heavens like a finger.

Fu rushed forward and Malao followed. The clearing was enormous and filled with a sea of stone monuments, which ranged in size from Malao's height to the height of several men. Though he had never been there before, Malao knew exactly what he was looking at—Shaolin Temple's famous Pagoda Forest.

"We made it!" Fu said.

Malao smiled. He looked back at the white monkey, which sat high atop a large maple at the edge of the tree line. The monkey made a quick motion like it was blowing Malao a kiss, then it disappeared into the forest. Malao sighed and looked at Fu.

Fu smirked. "Wasn't that precious."

Malao punched Fu in the arm.

Fu laughed. "Well, what are we waiting for? Let's go meet our new brothers! I wonder what they're having for dinner?"

Malao scratched his head. "Hey, do you mind if I do something first? It should only take a few moments."

"What could be more important than dinner?"

"I'd like to find the small pagoda built for the boy who . . . you know . . ."

Fu raised his eyebrows. "The boy who fell into the soup?"

Malao nodded.

"You're terrible, Malao. Haven't you joked enough about that?"

"No, no," Malao said. "This is no joke. Honest. I want to pay my respects. Will you help me find it?"

Fu groaned. "I guess so. Why don't we—" Fu suddenly stopped talking. He stood perfectly still and pointed through the Pagoda Forest.

Malao followed Fu's finger and saw tendrils of smoke rising into the sky. He strained his eyes and began to make out a series of rooftops behind a high wall. One or two looked charred and broken.

"A big fire?" Malao said.

"Shhh!" Fu whispered. "More like an attack, I think. Just like Cangzhen."

"No way," Malao said. "This is *Shaolin* Temple. Nobody could—"

"Quiet!" Fu whispered. "The enemy might be all around us."

Malao rolled his eyes. "You're paranoid, Pussycat."

"Oh, yeah? Where are all the monks?"

"It's the middle of the afternoon," Malao said. "If this were Cangzhen, it would be nap time. You remember nap time, don't you?"

"Keep your voice down!" Fu whispered. "It's better to be safe than sorry."

"Fine," Malao whispered. "What do you suggest we do?"

"Let's split up." Fu pointed to a tall oak behind Malao. "You climb that tree and keep an eye out while I sneak up to the compound and investigate. If you see anything suspicious, screech like a monkey. Otherwise, stay quiet and sit tight. I'll come back here as soon as I'm through."

Without another word, Fu turned and sprinted over to a large six-sided pagoda. After quickly scanning the area, he ran and dove next to a smaller one with a rectangular base. A moment later, Malao lost sight of him.

Malao shrugged his shoulders and walked to the tree Fu had singled out. He stretched and casually leaped toward the thick trunk—but felt himself suddenly yanked back to earth. A firm hand slithered over his mouth and clamped down hard enough to bruise his lips.

A familiar voice hissed in his ear, "Silly little monkey. You should learn to listen to your older brothers."

CHAPTER 29

Malao knew there was no point in fighting back. He relaxed and the hand over his mouth slipped away, dragging a thin line of saliva across his cheek.

"That's disgusting," Seh said. He took a step back and wiped his hand on the corner of his blue silk robe.

"That's what you get for sneaking up on me like that again," Malao replied. "Can't you just say hello like a normal person?"

"Keep your voice down," Seh whispered.

Malao wiped his cheek and looked up at his tallest brother. He noticed Seh's spiky black hair was longer than his and appeared to be growing in unevenly.

"Hey, what happened to your hat?" Malao asked. "Maybe you should put it back on. It looks like your head got too close to Fu when he was practicing with his tiger hook swords."

"Stop goofing around," Seh said. "This is serious. I overheard you talking to Fu, and he is right. The enemy could still be near."

"What enemy?" Malao asked. "And by the way, what are *you* doing here?"

"That's a really long story," Seh replied.

Malao rolled his eyes. "Oh, come on—"

"Shhh," Seh whispered. "The bandits heard about a planned attack on Shaolin and I volunteered to warn the monks, okay? Obviously, I arrived too late."

"When did you get here?"

"This morning."

"Do you know who did this?"

"The rumor was a huge platoon of soldiers led by one of the Emperor's generals. But I don't know for sure. I haven't found anyone alive to ask."

Malao lowered his head. "This is terrible."

"You have no idea how terrible," Seh said. "It's awful back inside the Shaolin compound. Is that where Fu is headed?"

"Yeah."

"He's in for an unpleasant surprise. I better go see if I can catch him."

"Wait a moment," Malao said. "Have you seen Hok?"

Seh's narrow eyes widened. "Hok? No. Why?"

"He told me and Fu that he would meet us here. But that was eleven or twelve days ago. The plan was for him to come here first, and then Fu and I would meet up with him later. Ying stole the dragon scrolls from Fu, but then we stole them back again."

"You guys stole the scrolls back?"

"Sort of," Malao said. "We got three. Ying still has one."

Seh patted Malao's fuzzy head. "Nice work, little brother. Did you happen to see Long?"

"No. How about you?"

"I still haven't seen him, either," Seh replied. "I'm sure he's fine, though. Listen, I want to catch up with Fu before he gets to the gates. Why don't you climb the tree like Fu suggested? We'll come back for you soon."

"Why can't I come with you?" Malao asked.

"Having a lookout is a really good idea, Malao. It's an important job."

"But what am I supposed to look out *for*? You already said you haven't seen anyone."

"Please climb the tree, Malao."

Malao pouted. "Fine. I'll be waiting up there. Alone."

"Thanks," Seh said. He spun around and headed straight into the Pagoda Forest without bothering to sneak around like Fu had done.

That's funny, Malao thought. *Seh doesn't look too concerned about staying hidden. Why should I sit in a tree while he and Fu get to look around? I have something important I'd like to check out, too. And it shouldn't take long to find it. I could probably take a look and be back in the tree long before those two return.*

After making sure Seh was out of sight, Malao raced around the Pagoda Forest scanning only the smallest monuments. There were nearly two hundred pagodas in the forest, but it didn't take him long to search just the small ones. Unfortunately, he didn't find what he was looking for—the pagoda dedicated to the boy who fell into the soup. Malao began to wonder if there was another group of pagodas somewhere nearby. Or perhaps the boy's memorial was placed off to the side, away from the grown-ups'? Malao scampered into the surrounding tree line.

About twenty paces in, Malao came to a small clearing bordered on three sides by a wall of thick vegetation. A heavy patchwork of vines hung from the treetops all the way to the ground. The snarled mess appeared to stretch well into the bowels of the forest.

From the edge of the tangle came a calm, smooth voice.

"Hello, little one."

Malao jumped. He looked up and saw a slender bald man in an orange monk's robe lying sprawled along a large branch high off the ground. The monk appeared to be about thirty years old and seemed very comfortable up there. One arm and one leg dangled lazily in midair.

"Who are you?" Malao asked.

"Who am I?" the monk purred. "I believe the question is, who are you? And, maybe more importantly, who is the tall one in blue?"

"He's my brother," Malao said. "We're monks from Cangzhen Temple."

The monk's bushy black eyebrows raised up. "Cangzhen? You're so . . . young. What are you doing here?"

"Our temple was destroyed and we need help," Malao said. "But it doesn't look like there's anyone left here who could help us. Well, except for you, I guess. What happened?"

"Two days ago Shaolin was attacked by soldiers," the monk replied. "Soldiers with *qiang*s. Thousands of soldiers fell in the battle, along with every single warrior monk. I am all that is left."

Malao felt his heart sink. "Who would do such a thing?"

"Why, the Emperor, of course. He's the only one with enough power to accomplish such a feat. He didn't do it alone, though. He had help."

"What kind of help?" Malao asked. "Was Shaolin betrayed by a traitor?"

"A traitor?" the monk said. "I guess some people might call him that. He's been called worse."

Malao sighed. "Our temple was betrayed by a traitor. My former brother, Ying, returned and snuck soldiers into our compound. Those soldiers had *qiang*s, too. More than one hundred monks died."

"Really?" the monk said, scratching the side of his face. "That's a shame. It sounds like Cangzhen suffered the same fate as Shaolin. Except Shaolin's losses were far greater. There were more than one thousand monks here and, like I said, I am all that is left. How many escaped the attack on Cangzhen?"

"Fi—"

"Don't answer that question," Seh interrupted as he slipped into the clearing.

"Hey, what are you doing here?" Malao asked. "Where's Fu?"

"He's back at the compound." Seh stared up at the monk in the tree. "Who are you? Tell me your name. Now."

The monk yawned and blinked several times. "Didn't they teach you any manners at Cangzhen?"

"Answer the question," Seh said.

"Very well." The monk sat up on the tree limb and leaned forward with his forearms on his thighs. "Most people call me Tsung. Welcome to Shaolin."

Seh's eyes narrowed to slits. "Your name is Monk? What kind of name is that?"

Tsung cocked his head to one side and smirked. "Mandarin. Why?"

"I'm not in the mood for jokes," Seh said. "Why would people call you Monk?"

"Because I am one," Tsung said. "Do you find it surprising that you should find a man called Monk at a temple?"

"Don't play games with me," Seh said. "You know what I mean."

"No, I don't know what you mean," Tsung replied. "What were you expecting, a Cantonese animal name, perhaps? I'm from Shaolin, young man. Only Cangzhen monks have Cantonese animal names." He paused. "Well, only certain Cangzhen monks. Ones with a certain, shall we say, *history*. But you already know that, don't you? I'm sure Mong told you all about it."

"I have no idea what you're talking about," Seh said.

Malao looked at Seh. "Mong? Is he talking about the bandit leader? How does he know about the bandits?"

"I don't know," Seh replied.

Tsung grinned at Malao. "So, you've heard of Mong? Don't you find it a strange coincidence that he has a Cantonese animal name, just like some of your brothers from Cangzhen? What was the name you mentioned a moment ago? Was it 'Fu'? Tell me, little one, what's your name?"

Seh looked at Malao. "Don't answer him. I don't trust him."

"You don't trust me?" Tsung said. "But you are from Cangzhen and I am from Shaolin. We are practically brothers."

Seh didn't respond.

"Would it change your mind if you knew that I saved your sister's life?" Tsung asked.

Malao's eyes widened. He stared closely at Tsung and noticed a wound on one side of Tsung's face. It looked like a large bird had tried to peck his eye out.

"Hok!" Malao whispered to Seh. "He means Hok!"

"I know," Seh replied. "I see his face."

Malao punched Seh in the arm. "But he said our *sister*!"

"My ears work fine, too," Seh said. "You know how pale and delicate Hok looks. He's just jumping to conclusions."

Tsung grinned at Seh. "Am I?"

"Yes," Seh said, looking sideways. "What happened to your face?"

Tsung rubbed the spot next to his eye. "Hok and I had a little . . . misunderstanding."

"A *misunderstanding*?" Seh said. "Tell me what you know about Hok!"

"I know that *she* has a Cantonese name and fights like a crane," Tsung said. "She arrived here on horseback before the attack, badly injured. She spent most of her time sleeping." He paused. "She talks in her sleep, you know. I believe she mentioned you once or twice."

Malao saw Seh's eyes narrow to slits.

"He's telling the truth, isn't he!" Malao said. He punched Seh again. "How long have you known that Hok is a girl?"

"I don't have time for gossip right now."

"Gossip?!" Malao said. "I can't believe you! How come you never told me?"

"It was none of your business," Seh replied.

"None of my business!" Malao said. "What else do you know that's 'none of my business'?"

"That's enough!" Seh hissed. "We'll talk about this

later." He glared up at Tsung. "You said you saved Hok. Where is she now?"

"I wish I knew," Tsung replied. "Even in her condition, she fought bravely during the attack. She managed to escape, but she was in very, very bad shape. I've been looking for her ever since. Unfortunately, I'm afraid she may have crawled into a hollow tree somewhere and . . . well . . . just never crawled back out. When I say that I'm the only monk to have escaped the attack alive, I am obviously not counting her. I've given up hope of finding her among the living."

"What?" Malao said.

Seh seemed unconvinced. "Why should we believe you?" he asked.

"Because I've given you no reason to doubt me," Tsung said. He looked at Malao and purred, "You believe me, don't you, little one?"

Malao paused and scratched his head. Something about Tsung's tone of voice suddenly seemed different.

"I'm sorry I keep calling you 'little one,'" Tsung said. "I hope that doesn't offend you. If you would simply tell me your name . . ."

Malao twitched. He realized Tsung was talking to him in the same tone the bandit Hung had, right before Hung turned on him.

Malao covered his mouth with one hand and whispered to Seh, "I think we should get out of here—"

Tsung sprang out of the tree and slammed into

Malao's chest. Malao found himself pinned to the ground with Tsung sitting on his midsection. Tsung grabbed the front of Malao's robe with one hand and formed a perfect leopard fist with the other. He brought his straightened fingers together and curled them down and in at the first two knuckles. Tsung cocked the fist back as Malao wiggled and squirmed.

Seh spun around and lashed out at Tsung's head with a powerful roundhouse kick. Malao's eyes widened when he saw Tsung duck the kick with plenty of time to spare.

Nobody is that fast, Malao thought.

Seh followed up with a lightning-quick side-kick. Again, Tsung dodged it easily. Only this time he twisted to one side and Malao's robe was yanked open. The two dragon scrolls Malao carried fell to the ground, along with the decorated stick.

"What's this?" Tsung said.

Malao reached for one scroll while Seh dove for the other.

In a series of movements so fast Malao barely saw them, Tsung snatched up both scrolls and raced back up the tree. Malao was left with nothing but a handful of dirt. Seh held nothing but air.

Tsung plopped down on the same limb and slipped one of the scrolls into his robe. He whipped open the other scroll. "Very interesting," he said calmly.

Malao rubbed his eyes and stared up at Tsung. He couldn't believe what he had just seen. As he picked up his stick and returned it to the folds of his robe, Seh laid a hand on his shoulder.

"I think we're in trouble," Seh whispered.

Malao nodded.

The sound of snapping branches caught Malao's attention and he turned to see Fu burst into the small clearing.

"What's going on here?" Fu demanded.

Tsung looked down at Fu. He shook his head and went back to reading the scroll.

Fu looked up at Tsung, then over at Seh. "Who is that guy?"

"He's a traitor," Seh said, glaring up at Tsung. "He's responsible for the destruction of Shaolin."

"What!" Fu roared. He looked up at Tsung. "Get down here, you coward! Fight like a— Hey! He's got one of the dragon scrolls!"

"Actually, he has both of mine," Malao said.

Tsung looked up. "What was that? Both of *yours*?" Tsung stuffed the open scroll inside his robe and pulled his feet up onto the limb. He sat back on his haunches and turned toward Fu. "What secrets do *you* keep, big boy?"

Fu growled and tightened his sash. Malao saw every muscle in Fu's body begin to tense.

"Wait!" Malao said to Fu. "You don't understand. That guy—"

Tsung leaped out of the tree and hit Fu so fast, Fu didn't even have time to bring his hands up. A perfectly formed leopard fist struck Fu square in the left temple and Fu crumpled to the ground. Malao and Seh raced to Fu's side, but by the time they made the five steps it took to get there, Tsung had already reached into Fu's robe, removed the third scroll, and raced back up the tree.

Malao and Seh stared at each other in disbelief. Together they looked up at Tsung.

Tsung grinned and placed the third dragon scroll inside his robe with the other two. He yawned. "So, which one of you two would like to die first?"

Malao shuffled his feet, speechless for the first time ever. He looked at Seh. Seh's eyes narrowed.

A voice suddenly rang out from high in the trees behind Malao.

"Well, well. If it isn't Spot, the Emperor's favorite pet. I see you're out of uniform again."

Seh looked at Malao. "Is that who I think it is?"

Malao took a deep breath. "Uh-huh."

Malao whipped his head around and saw Ying perched high atop a dead oak.

Tsung looked over at Ying from atop the limb. "That's General Tsung to you, Lizard Boy. And I'll wear whatever I please, whenever I please. What are you doing here?"

"I might ask you the same question," Ying replied. "Where are your men?"

"They're off getting some well-deserved rest," Tsung said. "Have you come to learn how a real man handles an attack on a warrior monk temple?"

Ying sneered and pointed to Malao, Seh, and Fu. "I came for the boys. I had no idea you planned to duplicate my attack on Cangzhen."

"Duplicate?" Tsung said. "I destroyed *all* of my former brothers. It looks to me like a few of yours not only escaped, they managed to make off with some valuable documents."

Ying scowled.

Tsung grinned. "Don't fret, young man. I'm here to help. Look." Tsung removed the open scroll he had stuffed in his robe. He straightened it out and began to roll it up. "I have two more besides this one. You want them?"

"Yes—"

"Then come get them!" Tsung growled. He finished rolling the third scroll and returned it to his robe. He tightened his sash. "I've heard stories about your fighting skills, boy. People are starting to say that you are in the same league as me. Apparently, they need to be reminded that I am in a league of my own."

Ying laughed. "You don't stand a chance, Spot."

Tsung paused. He cocked his head to one side and stared off into the forest beyond Ying. "Are those your men I hear coming?"

"Yes," Ying replied. "Are you going to scamper away?"

"Not at all," Tsung purred. "I was hoping for an audience."

THWACK!

Malao turned to see five armed soldiers hacking their way into the clearing with large machetes. They lined up beneath Ying.

"You men are just in time for the main event," Ying said to the group. "Where are the others?"

"Fanning out over various sections of the Shaolin compound and surrounding area, sir," one of the soldiers reported. "Commander Woo is determined to seal off all possible escape routes."

"Excellent," Ying said. He turned to face Tsung. "Is this a large enough audience for you?"

Tsung smiled and nodded.

Ying spat and spread his arms wide. "Then let the games begin!"

Ying swooped down from the tree and Tsung sprang into the air. They collided with an impact so powerful, Malao felt the percussion several paces away. Within moments, the fight reached a level of ferocity Malao had never imagined possible. Both combatants were out for blood. Malao noticed that Tsung was definitely faster, but Ying was much stronger. Ying never seemed to be able to connect solidly with Tsung, and Tsung's quick jabs had little or no effect on Ying. Malao knew it was going to be a long fight. He dropped to his knees, next to Fu.

Seh leaned over and whispered, "What are you doing?"

"Trying to think of a way to wake Fu up so we can get out of here."

"Good idea," Seh said. "Listen, I just thought of a plan, but it doesn't involve you or Fu. If you see me get knocked down, don't try to wake me up. I'll be playing dead. Understand?"

Malao nodded.

"Hey!" one of the soldiers shouted, shaking his spear. "What are you two talking about?"

Seh stood and walked over to the man. "None of your business," Seh said defiantly. He shoved the soldier hard.

"Why, you little—" The soldier lunged at Seh with his spear. Seh slid backward, easily avoiding the razor-sharp tip.

"You call that an attack?" Seh said with an arrogant laugh. "You fight like an old woman."

"ARRRGH!" The soldier rushed forward, lunging with the spear again. Seh slid back farther this time, almost to the very center of the clearing. He stuck out his tongue and the soldier swung the spear at Seh's head. Malao knew Seh could have easily gotten out of the way in time, but he hesitated before ducking. The spear shaft glanced off the back of Seh's head and he slithered to the ground.

Malao giggled softly and glanced over at Ying and Tsung. They were still in the heat of battle. As Malao turned his attention back to Fu, he caught a glimpse of Ying swiping at Tsung's legs with his long toenails. That gave Malao an idea.

Fu was lying on his back, so Malao sat down on Fu's chest and placed one of his bare feet on each of Fu's chubby cheeks. Nothing happened. Determined to wake Fu, Malao began to slap Fu's cheeks with his smelly feet. Still nothing. Desperate, Malao brought his feet together and rested them both on top of Fu's mouth. He wiggled all ten toes directly under Fu's nose. Fu's whole body jerked violently. Fu's mouth slipped open and Malao felt Fu's tongue slide across the bottom of his feet.

Fu's eyes snapped open. He grabbed both of Malao's ankles and yanked Malao off his chest. "What are you doing?!" he shouted. He sat up and spat.

The entire line of soldiers began laughing. Fu stood, red-faced, and looked around. "What's going on?"

"You were knocked unconscious," Malao said. "You wouldn't wake up and—"

"ARRRGH!"

Malao turned and saw Ying slam Tsung to the ground.

"Ying!" Fu said. "When did he get here?"

"Just now," Malao said.

"But if he's here already, that means my father is probably . . ." Fu's voice trailed off.

Malao's eyes widened. "That doesn't mean anything, Fu! It's been ten days since we left the village. A lot could have happened since then. Maybe he's fine."

"Or maybe he's dead!" Fu roared. He pointed at Ying and tensed every muscle in his body. "*You're mine!*"

Malao grabbed Fu's thick arm. "Fu, don't!"

Fu hesitated. He pointed to a pile of blue silk in the center of the clearing next to Ying and Tsung.

"Is that *Seh*?" Fu asked.

"Uhhh . . . yes," Malao replied. "But—"

"Nobody does that to *my* family!" Fu roared.

"Fu, wait—"

Fu charged straight at Ying and Tsung. Malao watched with his mouth wide open.

Fu unleashed a mighty tiger-claw swipe at the back of Ying's neck. Ying must have sensed it coming because he leaped off to one side. Fu's powerful fingers slammed into the front of Tsung's shoulder and raked downward on an angle across Tsung's chest. Tsung's robe was torn open and all three dragon scrolls tumbled out.

Before the scrolls even hit the ground, Seh sat up, whipped his body around, and snatched the scrolls with both hands.

Ying shrieked and lunged toward Seh, but Fu spun around and planted a brutal snap kick square in the center of Ying's diaphragm. Ying doubled over and Tsung leaped onto Ying's back, wrapping his legs around Ying's midsection and his arms around Ying's neck. Malao saw Tsung twist his body powerfully to one side, hurling both himself and Ying to the ground.

"GO!" Seh shouted as he stood. He slipped off into a thick tangle of vines. Fu hesitated, then put his head down and barreled into the dense foliage after Seh.

"Get them!" one of the soldiers shouted.

"Wait!" another warned. "Look!"

Malao turned and saw Tsung latched on to Ying's back with an unorthodox choke hold. Malao had never seen anything like it before. Tsung's arms and legs were intertwined with Ying's, and Tsung's forearm was wedged tightly against Ying's throat. It was without a doubt the most effective technique Malao had ever seen. Ying's face was red as a beet, and it looked like his head was about to explode. No matter how much Ying thrashed around, he couldn't shake Tsung. If Tsung didn't let up soon, Ying would be dead.

The soldiers began to close in and form a circle around Tsung and Ying. Malao made a break for the trees. With one powerful leap, he grabbed hold of a thick vine and swung toward freedom. When he was three trees into the forest, someone shouted, "STOP!"

Malao recognized that voice. It was Tonglong.

Malao stopped and spun around. He knew the shout wasn't meant for him, but he was curious nonetheless. He weaved his head back and forth until he had a clear line of sight into the clearing and waited. A moment later, Tonglong approached the circle of soldiers.

"Nobody touch them!" Tonglong said to the men. "Now back away!"

The soldiers backed away and Malao could clearly see Tsung still latched on to Ying's back. Tsung was panting heavily and his limbs shook from the pressure he was exerting on Ying. Ying's body had gone limp, but Tsung still held fast.

Tonglong drew his straight sword and rested the point against the side of Tsung's neck. "I suggest you let go, General Tsung. Immediately."

"Go . . . away," Tsung grunted. Sweat poured off his bald head like a waterfall.

"You have accomplished your goal, sir," Tonglong

said. "You challenged Ying, and now he's fallen to your hands. There is no need to kill him. Let go."

Tsung didn't respond. He held on like an exhausted man desperately clinging to the edge of a cliff.

"I will count to three," Tonglong said. "Release Major Ying, *or die*. One . . . two . . ."

Tsung let go and rolled off Ying. He tried to rise onto his hands and knees but collapsed. He didn't move again. Even from a distance, Malao could tell that Tsung had slipped into unconsciousness.

Tonglong knelt next to Ying, and the circle of soldiers began to close in around them.

"I told you men to back away!" Tonglong shouted. "Form a rank over there." He pointed behind him.

Malao watched the soldiers scramble to arrange themselves in a straight line. As the men hurried about, Malao noticed Tonglong lean over Ying and discreetly slip his hand into the folds of Ying's robe. Tonglong quickly removed a scroll and slipped it into his own oversized sleeve.

Malao gasped and Tonglong snapped his head up. Tonglong locked eyes with Malao and grinned. Malao twitched. He knew he should run, but he couldn't seem to tear his eyes from Tonglong's face. For the briefest of moments, Tonglong looked just like someone he knew. . . .

Transfixed, Malao watched Tonglong turn his attention back to Ying. Tonglong ripped Ying's robe wide open, exposing Ying's bare chest. Ying's rib cage rose and fell steadily. Ying was still alive.

Tonglong stood and adjusted his long braid. He pointed down at Ying and addressed the soldiers. "Look! The scroll Major Ying carried is missing. Did any of you see who took it?"

The soldiers all shook their heads.

"No one saw anything?" Tonglong asked. "Nothing?"

The soldiers all lowered their heads and shuffled their feet.

"What are you men ashamed of?" Tonglong said. His voice boomed. "Raise your heads and stand strong! None of you did anything wrong. I've been observing you for months now, and time after time I see the same thing—soldiers who are afraid to act. Men who are paralyzed with indecision. Men who have the right instincts, but are unsure of whether or not they should take action, so they do nothing. This is a problem. But it is not your problem. As your number one, it is my problem. And I intend to fix it."

The soldiers all looked up at Tonglong. Their eyes widened.

Tonglong sighed. "It is my opinion that you men are afraid to take action because you are afraid of failure. Unfortunately, failure in Major Ying's camp means punishment. We need to change that."

Tonglong made eye contact with each of the soldiers. "Gentlemen, I promise I'll do whatever I can to make your lives easier. In the meantime, we have some unfinished business. We must find the young monks. Now listen closely and take heed. We are sure to encounter many different creatures in the not-too-distant future, and each has unique skills. The leopard, for example, is the fastest and most agile animal in the forest, but it lacks stamina. Look—here lies one incapacitated after a few short bursts of energy. I am certain that ahead of us lie a monkey, a tiger, and a snake. The tiger can stay on the move for days and the monkey for weeks, but it is the snake that concerns me most. The snake does not have to run. It is a master of camouflage, and it strikes hardest when you least expect it. You have all seen firsthand how perfectly one played dead here today, only to strike when no one was paying attention. I suggest you keep your eyes and ears open at all times and watch where you step, for the snake now has the scrolls and we must get them back."

Tonglong raised a fist high. "Are you with me, men?"

The soldiers responded as one. "YES, SIR!"

Tonglong smiled and glanced back at Malao. Malao nearly fell out of the tree. He realized that when Tonglong smiled, he looked just like . . .

"Come on, little brother," Seh whispered from behind Malao. "Let's get out of here."

Malao jumped. He turned and looked at Seh. His eyes widened.

It can't be . . . , Malao thought. He glanced over at Tonglong, then back at Seh with his newly grown hair. Malao's mouth dropped open. "W-what on earth is going on?"

"I have no idea," Seh replied. "Now quit daydreaming. We have to get out of here. Fu is waiting for us."

"But—"

"Now!" Seh said. He grabbed Malao's arm and yanked him into the forest.

Malao looked back at Tonglong one last time.

Tonglong winked.

ACKNOWLEDGMENTS

I'd like to thank my editors, Jim Thomas and Schuyler Hooke, for their continued hard work and dedication to this series, not to mention all the weekend hours they put in on *Monkey*. Thanks, guys! I'm also grateful for the fantastic work illustrator Richard Cowdrey and graphic designer Joanne Yates have done on the series covers. Bravo!

Laura Rennert, my agent, deserves a tremendous thank-you for everything she continues to do for me on the business end and beyond, as does Barry Eisler, author, attorney, martial artist, and friend.

A significant portion of *Monkey* was written at Andy and Ruth Ann Anderson's cottage (on the lake!), so I have to thank them. I also need to thank my kung fu instructor, John Vaughn of Shaolin-Do, for his endless patience with my hectic schedule.

My parents, Roger and Arlene Stone, and my brothers, Joe and Jaysen Stone, never strayed far from my mind as I wrote *Monkey*. They definitely deserve a lot of thanks. I'd also like to say thanks to my "newest" family members for opening the door when I came knocking. That would be my birth mother, Sandra Kijorski, and her adult children, Scott McAlpine and Shannon Rumph.

The biggest thanks of all go to my wife, Jeanie, and our children, Tristen and Owen, who continue to support me in every way, day after day. I couldn't do it without you, Jeanie. Thank you!

Turn the page for a preview

of the third book in

The Five Ancestors series . . .

Snake!

PROLOGUE

€ight-year-old Seh slid his lanky body along the enormous rafter high above the Cangzhen banquet table, doing his best to disturb as little dust as possible. Even in a room as dark as this, Grandmaster would notice a single particle drifting toward the floor. Grandmaster was that good.

But Seh was better. As long as he didn't lose focus.

Once in position, Seh stretched to his full length and flattened himself against the top of the wooden beam. He began to slow his breathing. His heart rate slowed to that of a hibernating reptile beneath a sheet of ice. Seh began to wait.

An hour later, Grandmaster entered the room. Although Grandmaster didn't say a word, Seh knew exactly who it was. He sensed powerful chi—life energy—radiating from Grandmaster's body like heat from the sun.

Seh slowed his breathing further. He needed to keep his heart rate as slow as possible so that the chi coursing through his own nervous system would not alert Grandmaster to his presence. As long as he remained calm, Grandmaster would not detect him. Dragon-style kung fu masters like Grandmaster and Seh's brother Long possessed tremendous amounts of chi, but they weren't particularly good at detecting it in others. Snake stylists like Seh, however, were masters at detecting the most minute amounts in any living creature.

As Grandmaster stepped farther into the hall, Seh heard a second man stop in the doorway. Seh took a long, slow breath.

Seh focused on the visitor and noticed something strange. The man seemed to possess no chi at all, which was impossible. All living things possessed chi. This could mean only one thing—Grandmaster's visitor was masking his, something only snake-style kung fu masters knew how to do. And the only snake-style master to ever visit Grandmaster in the middle of the night was—

One corner of Seh's mouth slid down his long face in a lopsided frown. He peeked over the rafter toward the moonlit doorway and his eyes confirmed what the pit of his stomach already knew. Grandmaster's visitor was a man named Mong, a local bandit leader. Mong *meant* "python" in Cantonese. Seh had had more than one humiliating encounter with the gigantic snake-style kung fu master over the years, and he had no interest in seeing the man again.

Grandmaster turned to Mong and whispered, "Do you sense that we are alone?"

Seh remained perfectly still and watched Mong scan the room. Seh was enshrouded in darkness and positioned at a severe angle from the doorway. He was certain he was invisible. Yet when Mong's eyes hesitated as they passed over the rafter, Seh knew he had been discovered. Mong had sensed his chi. Seh was about to begin his retreat when Mong turned toward Grandmaster.

"Yes, we are alone," Mong said. "Nothing here but the occasional small pest." Mong entered the hall and closed the doors behind him.

Seh clenched his teeth. Pest? *he thought.* Seh wondered whether Mong was trying to make him angry so that his heart rate would rise and he'd reveal himself. There was nothing Seh hated more than getting caught when he was sneaking around.

Seh did his best to stay calm. He needed to stay focused. He suspected that Grandmaster and Mong were both dealers of secrets. They would trade them like other people traded gold for silk or silver for swords. Seh wanted those secrets. Especially if they involved him and his brothers—and Seh had a hunch they would.

"What news do you bring?" Grandmaster asked Mong. "And what might you require in return for sharing it?"

"I have no new information," Mong replied. "This visit is purely personal."

Grandmaster nodded. "The boys are progressing well," he said. "I suspect they'll all be masters in record time. Though I worry about the maturity level of some of them. Fu and Malao in particular come to mind."

Mong chuckled. "I imagine Fu and Malao could be a handful, especially if they're together. How is Long doing?"

"Very well," Grandmaster replied. "He is wise beyond his years."

"That's good," Mong said. "And what about the girl?"

"Hok is progressing well, too."

Seh nearly tumbled off the rafter. Hok? A girl? He took a long, slow breath. Mong was trying to break his concentration, and that last bit of information had nearly done it. But Seh was certain he could remain calm, no matter what Mong said next.

He was wrong.

"And what about my son?" Mong asked.

No . . . , Seh thought. It can't be. . . . He swallowed hard as his heart began to beat in his throat. He couldn't control it. He glared down at Mong, wondering if it was a trick.

It wasn't.

Grandmaster glanced up at the beam. "Seh is also progressing well. Perhaps too well. I worry about him most of all."